"I'm not baby-sitting you."

"I don't expect any special attention," she said.

Well, she damned sure had it. Rick took a step closer, grinning when she sucked in a quick breath. He allowed his gaze to linger at the level of her blue eyes, to saunter down to her ample cleavage.

"Excuse me," she said. "I'm up here."

Rick chuckled as he took his time making eye contact with Daisy. "Since I'm not about to spend the rest of my life helping you escape, let's set a time limit."

"Sounds reasonable. How about two weeks?"

He chuffed. "Do you think I've got nothing better to do? One."

"One and a half."

He wasn't going to win this round, and Rick Shane had a pretty good idea when to cut his losses. "Not a day more," he said.

Dear Reader,

Love is in the air, but the days will certainly be sweeter if you snuggle up with this month's Special Edition offerings—and a box of decadent chocolates. First up, award-winning author and this year's President of Romance Writers of America®, Shirley Hailstock is a fresh new voice for Special Edition, but fans already know what a gifted storyteller she is. With numerous novels and novellas under her belt, Shirley debuts in Special Edition with *A Father's Fortune*, which tells the story of a day-care-center owner and her foster child who teach a grumpy carpenter how to face his past and open his heart to love.

Lindsay McKenna packs a punch in *Her Healing Touch,* a fast-paced read from beginning to end. The next in her widely acclaimed MORGAN'S MERCENARIES: DESTINY'S WOMEN series, this romance details the trials of a beautiful paramedic who teaches a handsome Special Forces officer the ways of her legendary healing. *USA TODAY* bestselling author Susan Mallery *completely* wins us over in *Completely Smitten*, next up in her beloved series HOMETOWN HEARTBREAKERS. Here, an adventurous preacher's daughter seeks out a new life, but never expects to find a new *love* with a sexy U.S. marshal.

The fourth installment in Crystal Green's KANE'S CROSSING miniseries, *There Goes the Bride* oozes excitement when a runaway bride is spirited out of town by a reclusive pilot she once loved in high school. Patricia McLinn delights her readers with *Wedding of the Century*. Here, a heroine returns to her hometown seven years after running out of her wedding. When she faces her jilted groom, she realizes their feelings are stronger than ever! Finally, in Leigh Greenwood's *Family Merger*, sparks fly when a workaholic businessman meets a good-hearted social worker, who teaches him the meaning of love.

Don't miss this array of novels that deliver an emotional charge and satisfying finish you're sure to savor, no matter what the season!

Happy Valentine's Day!

Karen Taylor Richman
Senior Editor

Please address questions and book requests to:
Silhouette Reader Service
U.S.: 3010 Walden Ave., P.O. Box 1325, Buffalo, NY 14269
Canadian: P.O. Box 609, Fort Erie, Ont. L2A 5X3

There Goes the Bride

CRYSTAL GREEN

Silhouette®
SPECIAL EDITION™
Published by Silhouette Books
America's Publisher of Contemporary Romance

To Aunt Alina:
You are an inspiration and a treasure to us all.

 SILHOUETTE BOOKS

ISBN 0-373-24522-X

THERE GOES THE BRIDE

Visit Silhouette at www.eHarlequin.com

Printed in U.S.A.

Books by Crystal Green

Silhouette Special Edition

Beloved Bachelor Dad #1374
*The Pregnant Bride #1440
*His Arch Enemy's Daughter #1455
*The Stranger She Married #1498
*There Goes the Bride #1522

*Kane's Crossing

CRYSTAL GREEN

lives in San Diego, California, where she writes full-time and occasionally teaches. When she isn't penning romances, she enjoys reading, wasting precious time on the Internet, overanalyzing movies, risking her life on police ride-alongs, petting her parents' Maltese dogs and fantasizing about being a really great cook.

Whenever possible, Crystal loves to travel. Her favorite souvenirs include journals—the pages reflecting everything from taking tea in London's Leicester Square to backpacking up endless mountain roads leading to the castles of Sintra, Portugal.

She'd love to hear from her readers at: 8895 Towne Centre Drive, Suite 105-178, San Diego, CA 92122-5542.

THE KANE'S CROSSING GAZETTE

Beauty-Queen Bride Flees!
by Verna Loquacious, Town Observer

Greetings from your friendly neighborhood grapevine!

My, oh my. When she won the crown of Miss Spencer County, Daisy Cox was merely a senior in high school. Now she's "running" for another title— "Little Miss What-do-you-think-you're-doing?"

Ms. Cox was last seen sprinting from the Pioneer Square church, and rumor has it that she eluded her husband-to-be and his wedding guests by taking up with that no-good Rick Shane. Supposedly he flew her right out of Kane's Crossing in that tin can of a plane he owns!

Will Ms. Cox fall for Rick Shane's bad-boy charm? Read the next installment to find out…

Chapter One

It should have been the perfect wedding.

Through the misty haze of sentimental, goodbye-single-life tears, Daisy Cox clutched her $300.00 bouquet of orchids, the bodice of her Vera Wang original gown siphoning air from her lungs. Surrounded by thousands of dollars worth of lilies and roses, serenaded by the most expensive string quartet money could buy, she should have been walking on air.

Instead, she was choking on it. Especially when her gaze skimmed over her fiancé, Peter Tarkin.

She shut her eyes, listening to the drone of the preacher's voice. When she blinked open again, her husband-to-be was still there, as Dracula-dapper as ever, his midnight-black tuxedo and silver-templed coif at odds with the late-September sunlight dappling through the church's stained glass.

Silently, she willed him to step into the light. Maybe he'd turn to dust, liberating her from the worst decision she'd ever made in her entire, misspent life.

Daisy glanced at Coral, her maid of honor. Her big sister. Tears glistened down Coral's ruddy cheeks, and Daisy couldn't help thinking that they were tears of relief.

The preacher was on a throbbing-veined, ecstatic roll. "Love is a precious thing, a fragile blossom braving the cold of winter and the heat of summer...."

Daisy breathed deeply, calming herself, feeling the ten extra pounds she'd gained during the past two months straining against the satin of her dress. Do something, she told herself. This is the first moment of the rest of your life.

"Excuse me," she said, her voice a thin whisper.

The preacher stopped mideffusion, his mouth agape.

For a blind moment, Daisy considered pretending like she'd merely hiccuped. Then the ceremony could continue, everything hunky-dory, just as smooth and unruffled as a cup of cream. Just like Peter's life. But when her fiancé narrowed his eyes, reminding her that he'd pressed his fingers against her throat only this morning when she'd expressed doubt about marrying him, Daisy's spirit kicked her body into gear.

Today had been the first time he'd laid a harsh hand on her. And it would be the last, too.

She stepped up to the dais, facing the good citizens of Kane's Crossing. Daisy didn't know them very well, but from what she remembered of this town, they wouldn't mind if she did something stupid. Something that would stoke their gossip fires for the coming autumn.

Well, she was about to oblige them.

She cleared her throat and smiled, drawing on all her years of beauty-pageant experience. Walk a straight line—posture, posture—flash those pearly whites, swivel, pose... Once upon a time, she'd been crowned Miss Spencer County, and it hadn't been for nothing.

Coral was watching her, that you're-up-to-something-no-good-young-lady purse to her lips.

Daisy kicked up her smile a notch; it went from maudlin-sweet to Vaseline-bright. "I want to take a moment to thank so many people. Like the caterers. You all are going to love the shrimp salad and prime rib. And thank you to the wedding planner. Beautiful work, Adele."

As the planner waved and wiped her eyes, Daisy went on to thank every one from the photographer to the limousine driver, noting how Peter's brows were knitted. She'd seen that expression before, and she hadn't appreciated the threat that had accompanied it, hadn't appreciated how yesterday's verbal intimidation had become this morning's choke hold.

I wouldn't call off this marriage, he'd said one day when she'd confessed her cold feet to him. *You'll be very sorry if you do.*

Now Peter started to interrupt her, but Daisy cut him off, plunging into her final acknowledgments.

"Thank you to my sister, Coral, for loving me all these years, for raising me and making so many sacrifices. I love you, sis."

Coral smiled, deepening the crow's feet around her wary, faded bluebonnet-colored eyes.

"And, finally, thank you to Liza Cochrane, my bridesmaid." Daisy paused, her heart racing with nerves and anger, as she locked eyes with the woman Peter had insisted be in the wedding party. The woman her future husband had...

Just the thought of it made her want to cry with helpless embarrassment.

"Liza," she said, "thank you for sleeping with the biggest mistake I never made." Amidst a general gasp from the congregation, Daisy dropped the bouquet at her bridesmaid's feet, as if it were a used tissue and Liza was the missed garbage container. The arrangement landed with a thump, hammering home the silence.

Daisy didn't look back, not even when Peter called to her in his low, controlled tone. Not even when she heard Coral reassuring him that she'd return. Daisy merely strolled out the front door and down the stairs, skirt bunched in both hands.

When she heard the growing mumble of voices inside the church, followed by the cacophony of bodies rising to their feet, she quickened her steps. Then she ran.

Past Pioneer Square with its stoic Kane Spencer statue watching her skirts fly. Past Darla's Beauty Shop, where this morning she'd gotten her curls

tamed into a style that flattered her tiara headdress
and veil. Past Meg Cassidy's bakery, where her wedding cake had been fashioned by the town "witch's"
talented hands.

A Chubby Checker tune blared from the building,
and Daisy skidded to a halt, backtracking. Through
the window, she could see a crowd of people decked
out in party hats and smiles, hugging and dancing
amidst streamers and light.

Daisy peered down Main Street, recognizing Peter
as he marched out of the church, followed by a throng
of Kane's Crossing curious.

Without another thought, she ducked into Meg's
bakery.

Rick Shane thought he was losing his mind. Again.

He'd been standing in a dark corner for about a
half hour now, doing his best to distance himself from
the revelry of his niece's seventh birthday party. The
last thing he expected to find as he stared out the
bakery window was a buxom, blond bride sprinting
down Main Street, Cinderella dress hiked over her
knees to reveal shapely white-stockinged calves. The
part he liked best was when she'd skidded to a halt,
her ample breasts all but spilling out of her neckline.
Rick liked that part a whole lot.

Then he realized who this bride was.

The satin dream burst through the door, welcome
bells jingling over the obnoxiously joyful music. She
seemed out of place among his jeans-and-leather clad
relatives and friends.

Behind the service counter, Nick Cassidy snapped off the stereo system as everyone else stared at the bride.

She straightened, and Rick grinned as he recognized the stance from high school. He'd always gotten a good rise out of Daisy Cox's feistiness.

"Excuse me," she said, breathlessly. "May I hide behind your counter?"

Meg Cassidy guided her wobbly-legged twin son and daughter to her husband, Nick. Unfazed, she nodded. "Certainly."

"Thank you." Daisy Cox rushed behind the Formica structure, leaving the party in stunned, statue stillness.

Rick shook his head and laughed to himself. "Only in Kane's Crossing," he muttered.

His brother, Matthew, slumped in a nearby booth and kicked a cowboy-booted foot over a knee. Their friend, Sheriff Sam Reno, sat across from him. Both of them were biting back their own smiles.

As the rest of the partygoers watched, Daisy Cox disappeared behind the counter, leaving a trail of white satin as she tucked herself away. The material peeked around the corner, a dead giveaway to her location.

Rick shook his head. This was definitely the topper to his day. Not only was he surrounded by pregnant women—both Meg Cassidy's and Ashlyn Reno's waistlines were starting to pooch, and his own sister-in-law, Rachel Shane, was expecting, too—but now he had to add a bride to the list of love-is-in-the-air reminders. All these hearts and flowers were making him downright discomfited.

His younger stepsister, Lacey, pursed her lip-glossed mouth, darting a glance from Daisy's satin to Rick. Nice. He knew the look. It meant that she was about to tell him to get off his lackadaisical rear end and do something.

As she approached, Rick couldn't help prefacing her baby-sister bossiness with a zing of sarcasm. "Yes, your Flashdance-ness?"

Lacey adjusted her off-the-shoulder sweatshirt and frowned at him. Hell, he couldn't help it. It was too much of a temptation to poke fun at her ever-changing wardrobe.

"Rick, you were in the same high-school class as Daisy Cox was."

He pretended to turn the matter over in his mind. After a sufficiently maddening pause, he said, "I guess I was."

"Then go talk to her."

Rick could feel his sibling, Matthew, as well as the brood brothers, Nick and Sheriff Sam, staring at him. No help there.

He said, "We weren't bosom buddies, Lacey." Though the thought of getting to know the bosom part of Daisy Cox didn't seem all that bad of an idea.

Lacey shot him the look of instant death, the kind only a sister could get away with. "Rick Shane, you go make her feel welcome."

Meg Cassidy and Ashlyn Reno had taken on expectant expressions, too. Even Rachel, the sister-in-law who'd always treated him like an important part of the family—which he knew wasn't the case—started getting a disappointed tilt to her lips. That did it. That, and the curious glances of his niece, Tamela, and little Taggert Reno, the adopted son of Ashlyn and Sheriff Sam.

Jeez, he couldn't look like a jerk in front of the kids.

He aimed a lethargic shrug at Lacey, emerged from his dark corner and ambled toward the bridal satin peeking out from behind the counter. Someone had the presence of mind to turn on the music again so Fats Domino could softly croon over Rick's attempts at friendliness.

He leaned against the wall, arms crossed, peering down at the bride beneath the Formica. She'd drawn her knees to her chest, resting a chin on the gleaming material of her gown. Her tiara and veil had gone lopsided, almost lost in a swirl of blond ringlets.

A protective urge tugged at his heart, and he wondered why she'd been running down the tiny streets of Kane's Crossing in a wedding dress. This was a quirky town but, come on.

He thought back to high school, to a girl who'd rarely attended classes because she'd been traveling the state for her beauty pageants. He'd always kind of had the hots for her, had always wondered if a beautiful goody-goody girl like Daisy Cox would even give him the time of day.

But he'd never found out. After graduation he'd

run off to a faraway land and lost himself, leaving no room for idiotic fancies.

Daisy's voice brought him back to the moment. "I remember you. Rick Shane, right?"

The fact that she recalled who he was sent a jolt of nostalgia, of lonely hunger through his veins. He ignored the emotion, half-nodding to acknowledge her words.

"Daisy Cox." He drawled out her name, stretching it between them with the slow ease of a man slipping satin from a woman's shoulders. He liked the sound of it, the impossibility of it.

Her blue eyes widened for the slightest second, then narrowed a bit. There. That was a little more familiar. She'd worn the same expression every time he'd leaned against the Spencer High lockers and ushered her down the hall with a suggestive grin. She'd been hard to get, the girl voted most likely to be too good for a guy like Rick Shane. It had fed his fantasies all the more.

But that was before his life had changed. Before he'd been forced into manhood in a little country on the other side of the world.

"Hey, Rick," said his brother, Matthew. "We're gonna have company in a few seconds. Maybe you could pretend that you're having a conversation with something other than the counter."

The hard edges of a comeback curse lined Rick's mouth, but he held it back. Leave it to Matthew to act superior.

Rachel, his sister-in-law, smiled at him, cushioning

his temper. He stood away from the wall and bent to whip Daisy's dress out of sight. Then, as Daisy scooted over, he hunkered beneath the counter just as the doorbells tinkled.

Daisy gasped, probably from nerves. She shifted next to him, gathering her gown around her body as his arm pressed into hers. The contact felt nice, warm, soft, just like her spring-meadow perfume. Rick's body heated just by breathing her in.

Mrs. Spindlebund's voice creaked over the music. Rick could picture the elderly toothpick woman with her salt-and-pepper bunned hair and permanent sneer as she said, "Good afternoon," to the party.

Everyone murmured a return greeting. Daisy tilted her head, and a ringlet brushed Rick's cheek. He couldn't help thinking of the last time he'd felt a woman this close, breathing next to him, her hair tickling his skin. A twinge of longing shook him to the core, awakening a sleeping agony.

Mrs. Spindlebund continued. "I know you people are busy with important events—" there went that sneer during the word *important* "—but have you seen Daisy Cox?"

Rick could imagine his friends and relatives shrugging and tightening their smiles.

"Well—" Mrs. Spindlebund was, by now, probably fixing a glare on all present "—she couldn't have disappeared."

Rachel, who'd endured run-ins with the elderly gossip goddess in the past, had evidently come to the end of her rope. "Mrs. Spindlebund, we've been celebrating my daughter's birthday. Daisy Cox would have no interest in this party.''

''Very well,'' Rick heard Mrs. Spindlebund say. He could almost see the suspicion in her slitted eyes. ''And, Rachel Shane, don't think for one minute that Mr. Tarkin didn't notice your absence from his wedding today. He's your horse-farm partner, after all.''

Nick Cassidy didn't think much of nosy news hens, either. He asked, ''Can you blame a family for choosing their own kin over business, Mrs. Spindlebund?''

The bells on the door sang out. The elderly woman must've opened it, preparing to leave. Daisy relaxed against Rick, and he fought the urge to slip an arm around her, reassuring her with his touch.

Cut it out, he told himself. You promised you'd never get close to anyone again.

You can't afford to let down another woman.

As usual, Mrs. Spindlebund had the last word. ''You people think you're above the rest of us. What you did to the Spencers was unconscionable. You won't treat Mr. Tarkin the same way.''

Ashlyn Reno, a Spencer daughter who'd been disowned when her lawbreaking parents had left town, raised her own frosty voice. ''Don't let the door hit your bony bustle on the way out, Mrs. Spindlebund.''

After an emphatic ''hmph,'' the door clanged shut, leaving the faint aftermath of bells and the silence of an ended song.

Sheriff Reno's voice filled the emptiness. ''From my window view, it looks like the wedding guests are searching every building." He paused. "Ms. Cox, you're a wanted woman."

Rick glanced at her, watching as her face took on a sundown-hued blush. Long ago, he had loved to get her flustered, loved to see her flush and tilt up her chin after snubbing him.

But now, her reddened skin was more than a sign of agitation. It was the prelude to tears.

As one rolled down her cheek, Rick forgot himself. He thumbed away a wet globule from her skin and asked, "What the hell do you think you're doing?"

Daisy pulled back from his touch, burned by it, stunned by it. "I'm not going to marry Peter."

He must have sensed her discomfort, because he stood, casting a long shadow over her body, making her feel insignificant and petty.

When she'd first rushed into the bakery, she hadn't gotten a good look at him. She'd merely *felt* a presence in the corner—a tall, black shape that had lingered in her mind even while she hid from her problems. Now, as Rick Shane held out his hand for her to stand, she couldn't help remembering the high-school version of him: cocky, stand-offish, interesting in a cool, mysterious way.

For most of Daisy's life, she'd been a good girl. For most of it. But when Rick Shane used to lean against the hallway walls, a mischievous invitation in his eyes and a slow grin on his lips as he watched her walk by, she couldn't help wondering what it'd be like to be a bad girl, just once. Or maybe twice.

But Coral would've killed her. Her sister needed Daisy to remain a pristine beauty queen, competing in her contests and bringing home enough money to support them. Their parents had died in a train accident when Daisy was three years old, leaving her, the "surprise, late-in-life baby," without any close relatives to raise her. Twenty-year-old Coral had stepped in, working hard to keep their little family afloat. She'd even sacrificed her law-school scholarship to provide her younger sister with a home. Daisy couldn't forget that.

Even if it meant marrying Peter Tarkin to pay off the money Coral had borrowed from him. The loan that had helped them survive for years.

Daisy glanced at Rick once more. He was a man now, his sable hair brushing the collar of his long-sleeved shirt, his dark jeans traveling the length of his legs down to his boots. He was a walking shadow, a black cloud hiding thunder and a more explosive brand of mystery. Even his near-midnight eyes held shades of a wounded soul.

In high school, those eyes had been quick to laugh—at least, with everyone else but her. He'd always seemed to have a wink and a grin for the other kids back in those days.

The memory saddened Daisy, made her wonder why his smile wasn't as flippant, why the lines around his mouth seemed more like lost highways than rays of sunshine.

Obviously, he'd sensed her perusal. His jaw clenched, his mouth firmed out, his open palm dropped. It was as if an invisible wall had fallen around him.

On a whim, Daisy stretched out her hand, just to see if he'd respond. And he did, helping her up.

The force of his pull caused her to bump into him, her breasts rubbing against his chest. Goose bumps shivered her skin, every inch of it. She backed away—even if she could've used another breath of his spicy tobacco-laden scent—and adjusted her tiara.

With effort, she turned away, sighing, angling toward the partygoers, knowing she'd have to explain herself to everyone. "You're all very kind, helping me like this."

Behind her, Daisy felt Rick recede, probably melting into the shadows once again.

Aside from Rick, she didn't really know these people. A couple of them had gone to the same high school, but she really hadn't made many friends back then. She'd been working in pageants since the age of four and hadn't concentrated on her studies as much as answers to "How would you bring about world peace?" and "If you had a million dollars, how would you spend it?"

But she did know two of these people: Rachel and Matthew Shane, Peter Tarkin's horse-farm business partners. She'd met with them on occasion, when she was masquerading as the perfect hostess during Peter's dinners.

She sent a tentative smile their way, and they responded in turn. Phew. At least these people weren't angry about this wedding-day stunt she'd pulled.

She gathered her composure. "I guess I'm a runaway bride."

Ashlyn Reno broke into an appreciative grin, while everyone else plopped into the nearest chair. She asked, "Wasn't this supposed to be the wedding of the century?"

Daisy heard Rick's chuckle, and she darted an irritated glance over her shoulder at him. He was giving her one of those appreciative high-school glances, and she couldn't help the flutter of attraction that flew over her heart.

Ridiculous, she thought. *The last time Rick Shane saw you, you were thirty pounds leaner. He can't possibly think you're anything but an overweight bride stuffed into a satin casing.*

When she intensified her stare, he merely held up his hands, warding off her rancor.

She faced the others again. "I can't marry him. I don't know what else to say."

Rick's voice floated from the corner. "Maybe you could give us a reason?"

Everyone else's faces reflected his curiosity. And why shouldn't they?

She said, "I haven't even told my own sister why I'm not marrying Peter."

Meg Cassidy, the one who'd baked her wedding cake, took the children outside as the other women nodded in sympathy, encouraging Daisy to continue.

"Well, to make a long story short, my sister, Coral, gave up everything to keep us together as a family after my parents died. She was so young when she started raising me, and we struggled financially for a long time. I was a teenager when Peter befriended Coral. He loaned her a lot of money, especially when she got it into her head that I could be Miss America and we couldn't find adequate sponsors. It was expensive, but Peter helped us out.''

Here, Daisy could feel her blush intensifying, her tears returning to well up in her throat, choking her. She couldn't tell them about failing as a beauty queen.

Couldn't tell them about gaining so much weight that she would've been a laughingstock if she'd set a foot onstage. She'd lost the pounds, but never regained the confidence. Then she'd put on more padding, then shed it. Up and down, a roller coaster of diets.

Rachel Shane stepped forward. ''Tarkin can't force you to marry him, Daisy. The man treats you like a trophy.''

Rachel's blunt statement robbed Daisy of breath, of dignity, especially knowing that Rick had heard it. She didn't want to look at him, to see the loser image in the reflection of his dark eyes.

Daisy rested her gaze on the tiled floor. ''It's complicated. I have a duty to my sister. She gave up a lot for me, and Peter wants a wife more than our money, I suppose.''

No, she knew it was true; she just didn't want to admit too much in front of these strangers. Peter enjoyed the prestige of owning a former Miss Spencer County. He liked that she knew how to behave in front of guests, liked her ability to charm his company. She was a valuable business asset to an ambitious man. On more than one occasion, he'd referred to her as "a piece of art." In spite of the imagery, she wasn't sure if it was a compliment to be compared to a lifeless painting decorating his walls.

Rachel came behind the counter to place an arm around Daisy's shoulders. She met her gaze. "I believe you. However, Tarkin's not going to be happy about his intended wife leaving him at the altar."

"He's earned it with his infidelity." She took a deep breath, then exhaled. "But I'm afraid of what he'll do if we don't get married."

Rick's boots thumped as he stepped forward. His low voice brushed down her back. "What do you mean by that?"

A lump formed in her throat. She couldn't believe she'd been reduced to asking for help from people she barely knew. "He threatened me when I tried to call this whole thing off. Said I'd regret it if I did. And..." This was mortifying. "...I didn't think it would ever come to this, but he tried to hurt me before the wedding."

The moment slammed back to her. Peering in the church dressing room's mirror. Crying. Tugging the tiara from her head in an explosive second of rebellion. Feeling Peter's hand around her neck before she'd ruined her perfect hairdo.

Knowing that he'd been watching the entire time, lingering in the back of the room.

Daisy shivered, then stared at the floor again.

She peeked up when she heard the men rise to their

feet. Sheriff Reno stepped forward. "He won't touch you, Ms. Cox. Believe me."

Daisy heard Rick take a step or two toward her as well.

The petite woman in the ripped sweatshirt—it might have been Rick's sister—spoke up. "He can't get away with this. Daisy, what can we do for you?"

Relief welled over her. Coral would never believe that Peter had threatened Daisy; her sister thought the man was close to a saint for saving them with the loan. And she truly believed that Peter loved Daisy, not her status.

"I haven't actually planned this through," she said.

What could she do? Going back to Coral right now was out of the question. Daisy had no other relatives to turn to; that's the reason Coral had cared for her when their parents had died.

Wait. Maybe there was something she could do. A couple of years ago, when she'd visited St. Louis, a man named Harry Redd had offered her a high-class hostessing job at his prestigious corporate headquarters. She'd had bigger accomplishments in mind, maybe attending college to become more than a beauty queen, for instance. Her dreams had never materialized though, and she'd gained too much weight to even think of approaching Mr. Redd again. But if she could get in touch with him, promise to get in shape, secure a new life in a new city and send money to Coral to pay off Peter, Daisy might be able to live with herself.

She perked up. She could also contact a past-pageant friend who lived in the city, maybe even live with her until she could make her own way. Yes. This could certainly work.

"I want to go to St. Louis," she said.

She heard Rick's disbelieving chuckle. "St. Louis," he said.

Rachel asked, "Why there?"

Before Daisy could answer, the sheriff's wife popped out of her seat. "I have an idea!"

"Oh, no, Ashlyn," said her husband.

But she wasn't listening. "Rick's our resident pilot. He can fly you there, and fast."

Any optimism Daisy felt at this news was quickly squelched by the near growl from behind her.

"I don't think so," Rick said, causing Daisy to finally turn around to face him.

What she saw made her heart sink.

Chapter Two

Rick knew he looked like a piece of the devil's handiwork as he stepped into the light.

"You're insane if you think this is going to work."

Daisy's tiara wobbled to the side of her head as her gaze glued itself to the floor again. Her well-manicured fingers caught the delicate crown, righting it.

A protective urge flared to life inside Rick, but he tamped down the emotion. He'd never been very good at saving people. Didn't his family and friends know that?

But his friend Ashlyn Reno, a.k.a. former town troublemaker, was just getting started. Her husband, the sheriff, of all things, merely sat back in his chair, evidently willing to wait out this new storm of inspiration.

"Here's the thing," Ashlyn said, her eyes wide with daring. "The quicker Daisy can get out of here, the quicker she can get away from that old dried-up fiancé of hers."

"Ashlyn." Rachel half laughed as she chided her friend.

"I'm sorry, the truth must be told," she continued. "It's not a pretty sight when an arrogant old fool salivates over a woman half his age. In fact, that's downright disgusting."

Her husband cocked an eyebrow. "So you're willing to create a major Kane's Crossing scandal because you object to Peter Tarkin's drool?"

Ashlyn nodded, sending a saucy smile to the sheriff.

"That's my girl," he said, winking at her.

Rick cleared his throat. "As I was saying—"

By this time, Rachel had caught Ashlyn's hell-raiser bug. She smoothed a strand of light brown hair from her forehead. "I'm warming up to this. Peter Tarkin has had a reckoning on the horizon for a while."

Now it was *her* husband's turn to protest. Matthew said, "So the man disapproved when you ran our horse farm while I was away, and he's a bit of a misogynist, begging your pardon, Ms. Cox."

Daisy crossed her arms over her chest, as if warding off the truth. The whole town had gossiped about Tarkin's cavalier treatment of her ever since the engagement. Rick, busy hiding in his little cabin on the edge of Siggy Woods, busy trying to distance himself from life in general, hadn't paid the news credence. He hadn't really cared until Daisy had swept into the bakery today.

Not that he cared now, either.

As Matthew opened his mouth to continue, Rick tried to distance himself even more, especially since it was his big brother flapping his gums. The brother who couldn't even admit to hoarding their dead father's pride and attention. Not that Rick was bitter about it.

He cut across Matthew's words. "I think Daisy knows more about this town's history than you do," he said, referring to Matthew's recent bout with amnesia. Not more than two months ago, Matthew had returned home to Rachel and their daughter, claiming a loss of memory. He'd finally regained his senses, but he and Rick hadn't ever ironed out what had happened between them so long ago. On graduation day. Before Rick's time in the hot desert sun.

Something painful crossed Matthew's brown eyes and, for a second, Rick thought he actually might be able to communicate with his brother, thought that they could, someday, sit down and talk about the tension between them.

But Matthew drew his mouth into a straight line, ignoring Rick. "As *I* was saying, Rache, do you really think flying Daisy away is going to solve the problem?"

Rick flowed back into the dark corner, his pride stinging. Vintage Matthew, the favored son. He'd slapped down younger brother once again. And Rick had deserved it.

Lacey, the stepsister who could take control of a situation even in a torn sweatshirt that had gone out of style two decades ago, slapped her palm on the counter. ''I don't hear any other ideas.''

Daisy held up a finger. ''If I may say something?''

The room's occupants blinked their eyes at Daisy, as if they'd all forgotten the reason for their rambling. Funny, but Rick had been aware of her the whole time. Aware of her light scent, her gleaming curls, her smooth skin.

Snap out of it, he told himself.

Daisy straightened her spine, tilted up her chin. ''I believe St. Louis will do just fine. I even have a job prospect.''

Lacey gave her a thumbs-up sign. ''So if Rick can manage to fly me and the local businessmen to our meetings every couple of days, maybe he can stop being so stubborn about it and volunteer to help around here.''

What was he, a mercy chauffeur? ''Wait a minute. My Cessna's due for its service.'' Okay, so maybe he was stretching the truth a bit. His Cessna, his baby, was just fine. But all the same, ''I can't just up and fly out of Kane's Crossing at the drop of a cowboy hat.''

He shot a glance at Matthew's headgear, propped on his brother's knee. When his gaze traveled higher, their eyes met, clashing.

"That's okay," said Daisy. "I'll just take a commercial flight."

Shame suffused Rick's skin, marking him with stubborn rage. Why couldn't he just offer to help? Why couldn't he step away from his inner hermit— the one who liked to hide in that cabin by the woods—and be a savior?

Because he'd tried that before, and the results had been irreversible. Soul crushing.

Nick Cassidy finally spoke up from a corner booth, where he'd been watching Main Street from the window. "A commercial flight will make it easy for Peter Tarkin to track you down, Daisy."

Rachel spoke up. "But let's be fair here. We're asking Rick to put his life on hold while Daisy gets established in St. Louis. He wouldn't just drop her off and leave."

She glanced at him as if asking, "Right?" It smarted that his sister-in-law was even wondering.

Nick stood, his boots scuffing across the floor as he walked toward Daisy. "Here," he said, slipping a wad of money into her hand. "Whatever you do, this should keep you for a while."

Daisy shook her head. "I can't possibly—" Then she stopped, probably remembering that she wasn't carrying a purse. Besides, she couldn't go home now, not for money, clothes or apologies.

"No worries," said Nick. He looked at Rick.

Dammit. He'd always admired Nick Cassidy, especially with the way the man had cleaned up corruption in Kane's Crossing while empowering the citizens of the town. Having his friend watch him like this was almost as bad as having a big brother glaring at his wayward sibling.

Funny. He could almost bear that sort of attitude from Nick, but never from Matthew.

As Daisy stared at the money, biting her lower lip, Nick reached in his pocket again.

"No," said Rick, holding both palms outward, as if warding off an approaching enemy. "I won't need your money."

Damn. He'd just committed himself. He knew it by the way the women were smiling at him, by the way Nick and Sam were regarding him with a gleam of respect in their gazes. By the way his brother was nodding his head.

Rick averted his glance before Matthew could affect him.

Lacey swaggered over to hug him. "Rick's got that bulging trust fund from our parents, remember? Money isn't what makes him ornery."

No, life had made him that way. From their deceased parents, Matthew had inherited the horse farm and the Louisville business until he'd disappeared from Kane's Crossing. With Rick's blessing, Lacey, the stepchild, had taken over the business. Rick had only been bequeathed money—something that hadn't required brains or trust.

Subtly, so no one could see, he squeezed Lacey's arm and disengaged himself from her embrace. Then he walked toward Daisy. She watched him wide-eyed, just like she had in high school. Rick's stomach tightened, clenching with an unidentifiable hunger.

He hovered over her until she narrowed her eyes at him. Good, he thought. Don't depend on me.

"I'm not baby-sitting you," he said, knowing at the same time that he'd never be able to live with himself if he just plopped her in St. Louis and left her to fend for herself. Like it or not, his nature wouldn't allow him to abandon her, to take the chance that Tarkin would catch up to his runaway bride and make good on his threats to make her pay.

"I don't expect any special attention," she said.

Well, she damned sure had it. Rick took a step closer, grinning when she sucked in a quick breath. He allowed his gaze to linger at the level of her blue eyes, to saunter down to her ample cleavage.

"Excuse me," she said. "I'm up here."

Their audience stirred and started small-talking amongst themselves. Rick chuckled as he took his time making eye contact with Daisy.

"Since I'm not about to spend the rest of my life following you around," he said, "let's set a time limit for your St. Louis settling."

"Sounds reasonable. How about two weeks?"

He chuffed. "Do you think I've got nothing better to do? One."

"One and a half."

He wasn't going to win this round, and Rick Shane had a pretty good idea when to cut his losses. He'd spent his life practicing the art of fading into the background. "Not a day more," he said.

He backed away from Daisy and addressed Nick. "Might as well get this over with."

Nick nodded, and Daisy went to him, hugging him tightly. He accepted the gesture, fixing his thumbs in his belt loops as she stepped away.

"I'll repay you, Mr. Cassidy," she said.

Nick fought a grin. "It's an almost-wedding gift."

"Come on," said Rick, sensing the room temperature turning mushy.

As he moved through the baking room and out the back door, he heard Lacey promising Daisy that she'd bring her clothes and other essentials before takeoff.

He had to leave, before the women caught up to him, making a fuss about how he was so angelic and sweet for helping a damsel in distress. That was the last thing he needed, especially since he was a reluctant participant in the first place.

He opened the passenger door of his Jeep, removing the dog-eared flight manuals and greasy rags that littered the seat. Then he propped his body against the driver's side, lighting up a good cigar while he waited for the emotional farewell inside the bakery to play itself out. Damn, his friends and relatives loved a good drama.

He peered around, blowing out a plume of smoke. Kane's Crossing was Sunday silent, the backyards lining the rear of the bakery still and pious. The Jeep's passenger door was nearest to the bakery, so smuggling Daisy out would be that much easier.

His heart was actually pounding, dammit. Just as it had years ago, when he'd had much more dangerous things to worry about. A bead of sweat fixed itself to his upper lip and, with a lack of patience, Rick swept it away with the butt of his cigar.

Rachel and Matthew escorted Daisy out the back door, her veil and satin covered by a blanket. They helped her into the vehicle, instructing her to get on the floor so no one would see her. After shutting her inside, they turned to Rick.

Rachel kissed him on the cheek, and Rick tried not to flinch. Instead, he glanced away, tossing his cigar to the ground and driving it into the dirt with a boot heel. He didn't even bother acknowledging Matthew as he swept around the Jeep's hood and hopped inside the cab.

Once he'd started the engine and turned onto the road, he flicked on the radio, only to find a preacher blaring a sermon out of the speakers. He grinned, turning it a little louder, checking to see if the bundle of blanket, satin and Daisy would protest.

But the only response he got was the bounce of a golden ringlet as it worked its way from the coarse army-green blanket.

In a burst of mental gunfire, memory blinded him.

He saw another cowering female, desert sand burying itself in her hair like jewels in a crown.

Just as quickly, he shook himself back to the present, ignoring the throbbing pulse in his neck. His breath shortened, and he fought to regulate it.

But he couldn't steady his hands.

As he gripped the sweat-dampened steering wheel, he aimed toward home, toward a little cabin in the woods where, once, he'd been able to hide from the rest of the world.

Daisy wanted to ask Rick to turn off that darned radio.

No. She wouldn't push her luck. She'd been fortunate to find a way out of this wedding disaster, and she wasn't about to blow it by testing Rick Shane's temper.

Let him listen to fire and brimstone. Let him smile his cocky smile and try to get a rise out of her.

Daisy Cox was flying toward freedom, toward St. Louis, and nothing was going to stop her.

Under the blanket, she could pretend she was safe. Not like when she'd been a young girl, huddled under her comforter when Coral had told her that Mommy and Daddy were never coming home again. No, this time she was going to be reborn, emerging from this dark place with a new purpose, a new identity.

No more Daisy Cox, has-been beauty queen.

The Jeep shuddered to a halt, and she heard Rick's door open, then shut.

Seconds passed. Was that jerk leaving her here?

She knew he hadn't wanted to fly her anywhere. In fact, from the way Rick had protested his involvement in her escape, it was obvious that he'd just as soon strangle her for disrupting his life.

She felt guilty about it, too. Boy, did she ever. She didn't enjoy grinding weddings to a halt, inconveniencing her sister for the rest of her life or dragging a man away from his beloved existence in Kane's

Crossing. But if she'd had any other choice, she would have taken it.

Finally, her door swished open. "Are you *that* relaxed?" asked Rick.

She peeked out of the blanket's dark comfort, squinting as sunlight and Rick's irritation poured over her. "A gentleman would help me out."

"I *am* helping you out." He walked a couple of steps away, then paused. Shaking his head, Rick returned, holding out a hand.

She peered down her nose at it, then made her way out of the Jeep. She could feel her breasts working themselves out of her bodice, but that's what you got when you power ate before a big wedding. The seamstress had almost slapped Daisy silly when she'd shown up for her final fitting, ten pounds heavier than the last time.

And it wasn't as if she'd been a twiggy creature during the first fitting, either.

When she finally managed to get to her feet without Rick's help, she grinned at him. He stared right back, his face emotionless.

"Your crown is crooked," he said, then turned away to walk toward his cabin.

As she adjusted her veil and followed him, she couldn't help widening her smile. Freedom. Rick had it, with this cabin nestled on the fringes of a woodland copse. Pine trees guarded the solemn cabin with its knotholes decorating a cozy porch. All Rick Shane needed to be Davy Crockett was a coonskin cap and buckskins hugging his long legs.

Daisy sighed. She wasn't about to think teenaged-girl thoughts about Rick again. That was then, this was now. And now was a whole lot more stressful.

He opened the unlocked front door and gestured for her to come in. She almost refused, just to be contrary. Just to see him grin at her like he used to in high school.

But she didn't know if he'd respond the same way now. As a matter of fact, she wouldn't be surprised if Rick hated her guts for roping him into her mess of a life.

As she stepped inside, the smell of pine washed over her senses. It was a man's abode, all right, with patterned Indian blankets strewn over a spindly-legged couch, with woven mats serving as rugs and with a pillow-tossed, unmade bed resting in the corner. A T-shirt slouched over a chair back, trailing a pair of well-worn jeans that had found pooled sanctuary on the hardwood floor. It looked as if he'd stepped out of the clothing on the way to bed.

She could almost imagine him without a stitch of material covering his body, could almost imagine shadows playing over his hard chest while a rumpled sheet hid everything below. What if she slid that phantom sheet lower and lower...?

Stop right there, she told herself.

When she glanced at him, his brow was cocked, obviously aware that *she* was aware of the discarded clothes.

As if the sight of them was enough to unnerve her. All her life, she'd been paraded in front of judges, cheering parents, back-stabbing Miss So-and-so's. Did he think she was so easily flustered?

Daisy pasted on her best panel-winning smile. "I want to take this opportunity to thank you for your help, Rick."

Hmmm. She shouldn't have said his name. It seemed far too intimate in light of the tossed-away jeans.

He must have possessed nerves radar, because just as soon as she thought "Hmmm," he started moving toward her, shadowing her with his long body.

"Don't thank me now. We've got a ways to go, darlin'."

Daisy swallowed, coating her suddenly dry throat with indifference. "Well, it needed to be said."

Well? The word was a time buyer, a dead giveaway to a loss of composure.

He took a step closer, bringing with him the slight scent of tobacco. Closer, close enough so she could see the outline of his Adam's apple against a corded throat.

Close enough so his low voice rained through her with a liquid vibration. "You actually think this hare-brained plan is going to work?"

He reached out, grasping her blanket with both hands, the heat from his fingers making the skin of her throat tingle.

"It's got to work." Oh, she sounded scared, desperate.

Nervous.

He tugged the coarse material off her shoulders, her

veil whispering against it. Cold air hit her chest, and she peered downward, realizing how much cleavage was exposed. She shifted, hoping he wasn't as aware of it as she was.

His voice softened. "You really think Tarkin is coming after you."

It was a statement, not a question. She remembered Peter's face when he'd threatened her in his oh-so-silky way. Remembered his fingers, tightening, cutting off her gulp of surprise.

"Yes, he will," she said.

Rick floated a dark glance over her shoulder, and she couldn't help thinking that there was more to him than just being a black-sheep layabout.

When had he changed from a lean-against-the-lockers kid to this dark cloud?

He was looking at her again. Not at her breasts, but into her eyes, as if searching for an answer he'd never find. He reached out once more.

She wanted to rear back, but couldn't. The good girl still wanted to be touched by the bad boy. She wanted to kick off the white-satin shoes and dance around in red stilettos.

She didn't move.

Gently, he skimmed a hand over her veil, stopping when he came to the tiara. She felt bobby pins being loosened from her hair as he worked them free, and she closed her eyes, feeling the room spin. Then, finally, the weight of the accessory disappeared.

When she opened her eyes, he cradled the faux diamonds in his hands, almost like a man cupping a woman's face before he whispered promises to her. The moment slowed, lasting a short infinity, before he grinned and tossed the tiara on the couch.

Then he focused on her again, his gaze hungry enough to put the fear of a good girl back into her soul.

He said, "Have you ever been to St. Louis?"

"Yes." Croak.

"Not a safe place."

As he moved forward, she moved back. Straight into the wall. He caged her between his muscled arms, leaning a lace-veil's breath away from her lips.

She controlled her breathing, her hopscotch heartbeat, trying to keep calm, trying not to appear rattled. "St. Louis is where I'll find a new life. Freedom."

The word rang between them, as fleeting as a fear-driven skip of the pulse.

"You're running away from your problems, Daisy." His breath warmed her mouth, tingling her lips with thoughts of what might come next.

Daisy. The way he said her name made her want to run her fingers over his chest, to dip them into the tight space between his shirt and waistband. "I'm doing the right thing," she said.

She didn't know how she was even able to speak, what, with this loss of breath. When Rick was near, it was almost like running through rarefied air. She couldn't help being light-headed and weak-kneed.

How could this even be happening? Didn't Rick realize that the woman he had trapped in his arms wasn't the same as she was in high school? Hadn't he noticed that she was layered with a protective coat of chub these days?

Evidently, he was blind.

But he was still moving closer, his lips brushing over hers. "You'd better hope you're doing the right thing," he said, tickling the skin around her mouth with the heat of his words.

Before she could answer, he'd leaned down and pressed his lips against hers, his mouth soft as a flame's curve, hinting at an element of danger.

Daisy heard herself moan low in her throat, heard it echoing down the halls of her heart. The sound slipped down her skin like the caress of a wilted rose petal, lost and fallen.

As she rubbed closer to him, her breasts crushed against his hard chest, satin and skin against the rough cotton of his shirt, wisping against each other with the easy rhythm of a fulfilled wish.

So this was what it felt like to kiss Rick Shane. This was what it felt like to wrap yourself in a rebel's leather jacket, waving goodbye to your astonished friends and your past morals. His mouth felt so good on hers, so right.

Why had she resisted in the first place?

Though he still held her captive between his arms, Rick pulled back, depriving her of heat, a maddening grin on those lips. "Think about whether you're flying into more danger now, Ms. Daisy Cox."

Her heart slammed against her ribs as he increased his distance. She couldn't believe he'd just stopped, leaving her wide-eyed and cold.

He ran a hand through his wind-ruffled hair. "If you're still sure you want to go, use the phone to make your arrangements in St. Louis. I've got my own plans to make."

As he walked away, Daisy slumped against the wall, angry with herself for giving in so easily.

But it wouldn't happen again. She'd make sure of it.

Outside, after making his own calls, Rick clicked off his cell phone and convinced himself, yet again, that kissing Daisy had been a good idea.

Hell, half of him—the uselessly sentimental half— had given into those high-school hormones, kissing her because he'd always wondered what it would feel like. The more cynical half of him had only wanted to show her that running away from her problems in Kane's Crossing wouldn't end her misery. She needed to face them head-on.

At least, that's what he told himself.

His conscience slapped him upside the skull. Pardon me, but aren't you the hardhead who's been running from problems for most of your life?

Yup, he said to himself. That's me.

So practice what you preach, lazy boy.

Great. Now his inner voice was starting to sound like Lacey. After his real mom's death, and ever since Lacey had moved into the household with her own mom, Rick's stepsister had been a know-it-all. It was a terrible joke on him that she was usually right about things, too.

Even though she'd spent some of her childhood in a "home for disturbed girls," as her mother politely described it, Lacey had a better grip on reality than Rick did.

He shook his head, stuffing his phone into the back pocket of his jeans. He'd get by on his own judgment now, even if it killed him.

He returned to the cabin, hardly surprised that Lacey had arrived with a suitcase full of new clothes and toiletries for Daisy. The former bride was dressing in the bathroom, her wedding gown and veil abandoned on his dinner table.

Lacey met him at the door. "Okay. Daisy has called her contact in St. Louis, Harry Redd, and he's given the go-ahead for a job. One down. She also got ahold of an old pageant friend who's out of town until next week. That'll eventually take care of living arrangements. Two down. And, until then—"

"—Drive to Blue Grass for take off, etcetera, etcetera. It's all in a day's work for us mercenaries."

At Lacey's jaded stare, Rick tweaked his sister's nose. "I know what to do."

She shooed his finger away. "I'm just covering all the bases."

"As usual. Don't you have a business to run or something?"

She sighed, evidently put out by his lazy attitude. "I'm worried, Rick. We're dealing with a man who has connections. And he threatened her."

He didn't want to stress out his stepsister. She'd gone through too much in her short life to deal with that. In fact, during their younger years, Rick had made it a priority to shield her from insults and teasing. "Hey, don't think twice about us. We're big kids, Lacey."

Her gray-blue eyes twinkled. "Okay, wiseacre."

The bathroom door opened, and they both turned to find Daisy dressed in flats, roomy jeans and a baggy sweater. She'd washed away her makeup, her skin glowing, her baby-innocent eyes shining with the reflection from the blue sweater. Lastly, she'd pulled back her ringlets into a loose ponytail, curls framing her face.

Even in her modest clothes, Rick thought she was just as gorgeous as a bride. Her curves looked soft, feminine. He wanted to feel her beneath him, pliant and willing, just like she'd been during that kiss.

His body tightened. *That kiss.*

Lacey swept by him, clucking over Daisy. The other woman merely shot an irritated glance at him— not that he blamed her. He'd been damned forward this afternoon, and he'd liked it.

Seemed as if she did, too.

As Lacey grabbed the suitcase and led Daisy outside to his Jeep, Rick grinned to himself. Damn, he thought. I must be a real jerk for taking advantage of a princess in need of rescue.

He also knew he wasn't about to change, either.

As the women's voices faded, Rick wandered over to Daisy's forgotten gown and veil. He grabbed the items, tossing the satin over the couch. He worked the filmy netting from the tiara and threw it away from him, as well.

He stared at the crown, at the sun sparkling over the jewels. Then, his jaw tightening, he walked to a chest of drawers and pulled open the first compartment.

There it was, gleaming in the light. His past. His shame.

He settled the tiara next to his Silver Star medal and slowly shut the drawer, burying another memory.

Chapter Three

That night, on a lone stretch of small, remote Illinois airfield, Daisy stood outside the plane and pulled her sweater over her mouth, biting into the material. It was the only way to stop herself from using every cuss word she knew.

Rick supplied the language for her as he let loose a stream of curses. He clicked his radio handset back into place and glanced at her. "We're grounded for the night with that approaching thunderstorm. I'm not about to fly into poor visibility."

He stepped out of the Cessna, misted moonlight revealing mightily ruffled hair, spiked from the constant rake of his fingers. His aviator glasses, which had shielded his eyes while they flew out of Lexington, hung precariously from a shirt pocket.

As he spoke, steam from the chilly night mingled with the shaded air. "This place is a ghost town."

Daisy peered at their surroundings. Cornstalks lined the airfield, and an old road branched into the dismal horizon.

"We were almost there," she said, tugging her sweater's neckline away from her mouth and shrugging farther into her down jacket.

Rick wiped his hands together, staring at his silver-painted aircraft. Blue lines raced over the Cessna's curves, making the sleek high-winged plane a thing of grace. Daisy knew Rick doted on this machine; she could tell by the way he gently worked the controls, by the way he'd carefully touched down on this lonely airstrip.

He rested his hands on his lean hips. "You'll get to your new life soon enough."

Daisy bit the inside of her lip, holding back any complaints. Even if she was about to freeze her chilled cheeks off she wouldn't be an ingrate.

"Is your plane going to be okay here?" she asked, shifting back and forth from the cold.

"Don't worry." Rick grinned, giving the Cessna a fond pat. "She'll make it through the night."

Boys and their toys. Daisy wanted to roll her eyes except for the fact that this certain toy was her ticket to freedom.

Rick started to secure the plane and unload their baggage. "In the meantime, we need a place to stay. What's your pleasure? The Marriott? The Four Seasons?"

Once again, Daisy noted the bucolic landscape. "I'd settle for Mammy Yokum's shack, if it had a warm stove to take off the chill."

He chuckled. "It might just come to that, here in Armpit, U.S.A."

When he liberated her wheeled suitcase from the plane, Daisy clicked out the handle, ready to roll. Rick was traveling lighter than she was. All he had was a tattered duffel bag to throw over his shoulder. That and the equally worn bomber jacket he'd slipped into.

With one last glance at the Cessna, Rick jerked his head toward the mist-shrouded highway. "Ready for a walk?"

She would jog the rest of the way to St. Louis if she needed to. "Ready."

"Let me get that suitcase." He held out a hand for her to surrender it.

Once again, she felt the need to refuse his out-stretched palm. "No, thank you."

Rick considered her for a moment, his gaze running over her body, providing a heated trail that warmed her through and through.

"It's your party," he said, shrugging.

They moved out, and when they reached the road, her suitcase wheels droned on the asphalt and popped over gravel. After their unexpected landing, Rick had run across the old highway to a farmhouse to inquire about food and lodgings. The residents had told him about the nearby town of Broken Wing, less than one mile down the way.

One mile didn't matter, thought Daisy. This was an adventure, a new beginning. In a few months, she'd be thirty years old. *Thirty*. The end of an era. Thirty was when your bones started to creak and you lost touch with new music and fashion trends. Thirty was when you really became an adult.

Coral had lived with Daisy for so long that she hadn't actually been on her own. Thirty was a scary change. A welcome change.

As the moist, sod-laden air rushed over her skin, Daisy tried to regulate her breathing. It'd been a long time since she'd exercised. When she was on a diet kick, she'd do hours of walking and cycling. But ever since getting engaged to Peter, all Daisy had done was think of running away. In spite of the intensity of her wishes, the mental calisthenics never even shaved off a pound.

Now, as she tried to match Rick's long steps, Daisy could feel the wind being sucked from her burning lungs. God, she was out of shape. The reminder shamed her, but she wasn't about to admit her weakness to Rick.

As if sensing her troubles, he slowed down. Daisy flushed, wanting to sprint ahead of him to prove that she wasn't overweight, that she wasn't anything less than she used to be.

A signpost increased in size as they walked closer to it. Broken Wing, 1/2 mile, it said.

Rick peered down at her. "That's nothing."

She didn't miss the tacit question in his statement. *Can you make it, Miss Huff-and-Puff?*

"Good," she said. "I can use the exercise."

She'd meant it to be a joke, but somehow the flippant comment ended up thudding between them.

She was more aware than ever of his lean body, the corded muscles of his arms, while he'd looked over the Cessna. Why had she even put the subject up for inspection?

Rick stopped, and so did Daisy. The lack of sound from her suitcase wheels underlined his silence. When she peered over her shoulder at him, he'd all but disappeared in the shadow of the signpost.

"You look fine just the way you are," he said softly.

Right, she thought. But she didn't say it out loud. He had to be lying. After all, a guy who'd drop everything to fly her away from trouble had to have some kind of chivalrous streak, even if that guy was Rick Shane.

She heard the scuff of his boots before he emerged from the darkness. When he did enter the muted moonlight, he was expressionless, his eyes night-shaded and guarded.

She watched him walk past her, and she noted the joust-approach wariness of his stride. It was almost as if he moved with a shield in front of his body, the shoulder-slung duffel bag primed to defend against anyone who got too close.

When he noticed that she hadn't moved, he stopped. "We can rest."

"Do *you* need to?" she asked.

He grinned sardonically and shook his head, waiting for her to catch up.

Thank goodness he hadn't pursued the weight thing. When she'd come back to Kane's Crossing this year, after losing her spokesmodel job, most people had looked at her with pity. *Is that Daisy Cox?* their eyes seemed to ask. *The years sure haven't been kind to her, poor thing.*

Daisy knew she'd put on about thirty pounds worth of insulation since she'd last been in town. She didn't need anyone to tell her, especially since Peter had always reminded her that he wanted Miss Spencer County for a wife. In fact, he'd put off the wedding once because Daisy hadn't been in shape. Maybe it had been her subconscious at work. Who knew? But after the first wedding delay, Daisy had gained more and more padding, perhaps hoping the nuptials would be put off indefinitely.

It hadn't worked. Peter had merely hired a dietitian and decided that, after the honeymoon, Daisy would begin to aerobicize in earnest, whittling her body back down to her glory-day slimness.

There were so many reasons to run away.

Wind rustled through the cornstalks, slapping her cheeks with cold. She gave an involuntary shudder, though she wasn't sure it was due to the elements.

She wouldn't go back to the old days. Not for the world. Being slender wasn't worth the price she'd had to pay. It wasn't worth the tearstained look of guilt she'd seen in the mirror day after day, after eating too much and then forcing it out. It wasn't worth waiting until Coral would go to bed, then raiding the kitchen cupboards until she'd filled herself with so much food that she had to get rid of it.

Don't think about that, she told herself. Those days are over. You've got control now.

Rick's voice shook her out of the past. "There's something up ahead."

It was an eighteen-wheeler, the first they'd seen. They stepped to the side of the road, and Rick held out one side of his jacket to protect her from the rush of air and gravel as it roared past.

"Thank you," she said.

He shrugged and regirded himself with the duffel bag. When they stepped back onto the road, he spoke.

"I heard Tarkin has a place in Lexington. Why did he decide to settle in Kane's Crossing instead?"

Idle chatter. She wasn't sure he really cared, but maybe conversation would steer her thoughts away from focusing on her weight. "Peter wanted to settle in a small town. He said it would be a good place to raise kids."

"A real family man, huh?"

Daisy gave an unconcerned laugh, relieved that she'd never have to sleep with Peter. She'd been dreading the prospect, happy that at least he'd wanted to wait until they were married to consummate their union. "Imagine. Mrs. Peter Tarkin. I can't believe it almost happened."

Their steps had slowed, almost as if they'd chosen to take a walk down a country lane together instead of being stuck out here in each other's company. Even the mist had lifted a little, offering glimpses of dark blue sky.

Rick said, "You got yourself into a real mess, Daisy Cox."

"I suppose I did." She switched her grip on the suitcase handle. "And I can't believe it got this far. Maybe it started after I was crowned Miss Spencer County at the tail end of high school. I guess that's when I said goodbye to Kane's Crossing, hello to the world and the chase for Miss America."

Daisy swallowed. "Needless to say, my sister's dreams of fame didn't materialize. I lost the Miss Kentucky pageant." But she hadn't lost the weight Coral had advised her to get rid of.

Stop. She wanted to small-talk with Rick for the sole fact of avoiding the ache of her past. All she was doing now was bringing it back.

"So," she continued, determined to switch gears, "after the whole beauty-queen thing, I went from job to job, supporting me and my sister."

Rick's voice was rough, low, when he asked, "Can't she work?"

The question took Daisy aback. "She shouldn't have to. It was my turn to take care of Coral. After all, she never let me forget that she could've had a wealthy law practice if only she'd used her college scholarship instead of raising me."

"Sounds like emotional blackmail." Rick glanced at her, a hard look.

Daisy took great pains to avoid making eye contact.

"Don't say that. She gave up so much to make my life what it is."

Still, her justification sounded exactly like what it was. A justification. Coral could've gotten a job after the Miss Kentucky debacle. With both of them employed, they might've been able to pay off Peter Tarkin's loan.

But Daisy's pride wouldn't stand for it. She said, "Coral worked her fingers to the bone to put me through my pageants."

"You must've wanted to win pretty badly then."

No, she hadn't wanted that at all. One of Daisy's first memories came to mind. She'd won a children's pageant—she couldn't have been more than five or six—and instead of feeling happy about the crown, Daisy had looked at Coral's face in the audience. Her sister's pleasure had been worth every caked-on inch of makeup, every hour she'd spent rehearsing her little Liza Minelli showstopper talent song. Granted, Daisy's collective prize money had helped them get through the years, but it hadn't been enough. Coral had aided the pittance by working double shifts as a waitress, staying up late hours going over the checkbook to find ways of saving money.

But then Peter and his loan had come along. He'd remembered Daisy's reign as Miss Spencer County and wanted to sponsor her bid for the shiniest crown in the land—Miss America. After she'd failed even that, Peter had called in the money he'd spent on her. But Daisy had always suspected that her title's monetary value far exceeded the cash itself. The new king of Kane's Crossing needed a queen.

Had she wanted the glory badly enough to work her sister senseless? Daisy decided not to answer Rick's question.

Instead, she said, "We thought things would be okay when I became a spokesmodel."

She could almost feel Rick's caustic grin.

"Be quiet. It's a very legitimate line of work," she said.

"No doubt."

Silence. She waited for him to ask why she wasn't still spokesmodeling. Could she tell him that she'd started gaining weight again, and her employer had fired her?

Rick cleared his throat. "How does Peter the Great, the love of your life, come into the picture?"

She shook her head. "Coral and I knew we couldn't pay him back for his loan. But he said it didn't matter. That he wanted to marry me. You know, he seemed like a gentleman. He'd helped us in our time of need. Coral encouraged me, told me that maybe I'd return his feelings after a while."

Rick stayed silent, and she could feel the weight of his judgment.

"I wanted to repay my sister for taking care of me. And I truly thought I would be good for Peter. I'd be his perfect hostess and support his career." Cold, cold, cold. Had all the hours she'd wasted trying to decide if she could marry Peter come down to this? An ice-cold excuse?

She hadn't seemed so callous when she'd said yes to him.

She was so lost in thought that she didn't hear the semitrailer breathing steel behind them. She didn't hear Rick reminding her to leave the road.

She only felt the shuddering swirl of air suck by them as Rick grabbed her to safety, holding her in his strong arms as they darted into the cornstalks.

In the truck's aftermath, debris danced, lagging after the massive tires as the stale smell of asphalt and dust lined the night. Daisy and Rick breathed against each other. It wasn't until he shifted against her that she realized she was still wrapped in his protective embrace.

He was so warm under his jacket. Daisy allowed her fingers to linger on his rib cage just a moment longer, stealing heat, feeling the thud of his heartbeat.

It would feel so good to lay her cheek against his chest, to allow herself to rest and stop running from her problems for just a moment.

He tightened his grip on her waist, and she felt his body go hard. Her skin tingled, leaving her breathless once again.

When she peered up at him, his expression shocked her into a frozen second of fear. He had a bloodred moon reflected in his eyes, his mouth drawn as tight as a battle line. As she shifted against him, his fingertips dug into the small of her back.

She gave a tiny gasp of discomfort, and that seemed to break his spell.

He stumbled backward, as if someone had shot him in the chest.

Then, without another word, Rick Shane faded into the night, leaving Daisy to trail after him into Broken Wing, Illinois.

The road sign indicated that Broken Wing had a population of two hundred and three. From the looks of it, Rick thought that most of them were probably living in the nearest graveyard.

But at least the joint had a decent motel. And all Rick wanted right now was to sleep until the sun came up.

The Tuckaway Inn would do just fine. Located adjacent to a Swiss Chalet–inspired diner, the Alps cottages cuddled into the dream-fuzzed countryside. One car indicated that the Tuckaway had another lone customer. Or maybe the vehicle belonged to the apple-cheeked matron at the front desk.

Either way, it wasn't every day a man had the benefit of seeing cornstalks and gingerbread trim in the same blink. The past twelve hours were pretty surreal, but—then again—his life was getting more surreal by the minute.

Especially when it came to Daisy.

An hour after checking in, Rick stepped out of the shower, trying to think of something other than the runaway bride in the next cottage. Instead, he concentrated on combing his hair.

He knew his cut was scruffy—too long near the collar—but he didn't actually give a rat's hind end.

Not that he had anyone to care for about his appearance anyway. That was the advantage of living by yourself in the woods.

But the mirror allowed him the chance to look himself in the eye. What he saw disturbed him.

A man with a basalt-type hardness to his gaze. A man who'd been quick to grin in his youth, now reduced to a line-in-the-sand grimness.

There was a hideous slant to him. He could see it in the dark part of his irises, the part where no one cared to look anymore. It was the type of scar you couldn't erase, the type of ugliness that turned a decent kid to stone.

He faced away from his image, disgusted. Even Daisy Cox had brushed him off tonight when he'd told her that she didn't need exercise. That she looked just fine the way she was. She hadn't responded to his heartfelt compliment, had politely rejected him with her cool golden-curled finesse.

See, even Daisy Cox didn't want anything to do with him.

Hell, at least she could stand to face him at dinner. As a matter of fact, she'd done the inviting as soon as she'd seen that hilarious Swiss-countrified diner next door. What the hey? he'd thought. He needed food as much as the next man.

So after she'd gone to her own cottage to dry off and freshen up, Rick had done the same. Now, as he donned his bomber jacket, he left his room to wait for her.

As he scuffed his way to her cottage, he froze in

his tracks, held captive by a silhouette on the curtains of Daisy's window.

Good God, didn't she know that she was dressing in front of the window? Sure, the curtains were closed, but...

Good God.

She had the Rubenesque curves of an autumn-colored oil painting. Today, in a society of starving supermodels and "thin-is-in" brainwashing, Daisy stood out like a ripe strawberry resting against a bed of grass blades. Rick ached to run his palms over the swerves of her body, to pull her against him like he had on the highway, when the truck had zoomed in behind them.

Dammit, any decent guy would avert his gaze. Rick Shane wasn't halfway decent in the least, but he managed to turn around, to glare over the parking lot to see if anyone else had caught an eyeful of Daisy.

Empty, thank God. If he'd seen anyone out here watching her, he would've cuffed them silly.

Suddenly, he felt like a protector.

Cut it out, he told himself. You're not guardian-angel material.

He knew that most definitely. It had been driven home when he'd held Daisy by the highway, when he'd seen Clarice's ghost in his arms instead of the warm, vibrant Daisy Cox. Clarice's blond hair had misted away into the back of his memories, leaving Daisy's widened eyes, her parted lips.

And when Clarice had faded away, so had he,

stumbling away from Daisy as if a ghost had shivered through his body.

Hell, why was he even thinking about this? Clarice hadn't been in his life for years. His first love—like all first loves—was nothing but a saw-edged memory, jagged enough to still hurt.

Rick crossed his arms and dug in his boot heels, waiting for Daisy. He could never go back to Clarice.

And he knew he'd never go back to anything as bitter as love, either.

Chapter Four

Daisy found Rick waiting outside her room. He fit in with the wedges of shadow created by her cottage, rendering him almost invisible.

"Sorry," she said. "Didn't mean to keep you waiting."

She sensed, more than saw, his careless shrug. The only real answer she got out of him was the scuff of his boots over the blacktop, leading them both to the diner.

The eating establishment resembled something out of *Hansel and Gretel*. Fake icicles stabbed down from the shingled roof, and the gingerbread-brown paint job flaked away from the walls with anti-fairy tale disregard.

As Rick held open the glass door for her, he muttered, "Welcome to Paradise."

Actually, it was a bit like a dream. As she strolled into the diner's warmth, the pie-crust, baked-bread, French-fried aroma hit her full in the stomach, reminding Daisy that she hadn't eaten since this morning. She'd been too nervous to have anything but a bagel and cream cheese, and it hadn't sat well.

But now, the empty restaurant beckoned.

They took their seats opposite each other, in a tan-vinyl booth. Immediately, Rick grabbed a menu and sheltered himself behind it.

Okay. So he wasn't a talker. Daisy could handle that. She knew how to deal with all sorts of social situations with a touch of elegance. That's why Peter had wanted her, wasn't it?

Guilt washed over her. And what about Coral? How was her older sister doing? Daisy would really have to call her first thing when she and Rick arrived in St. Louis. Not that she was going to tell Coral where they were.

She sighed and scanned her own laminated food list. Oh, boy, she was hungry. And look, this place had all the calories a girl could ever want.

And them some.

Salad. In front of Rick, she should have leafy greens. Rabbit food. Prim-and-proper, girlie-girl grub.

From the way Rick had stuffed his own menu behind the double-sided napkin holder, he'd obviously decided on his own feast for the night. He'd also tugged a cigar out of his jacket and was busy patting down his pockets for a light.

Daisy set her menu aside, grabbing a napkin, flaring it over her lap. "You're going to smoke in here?"

He stopped all motion, glancing up at her with a sardonic cock of the brow, his hands frozen over his chest. "Yeah. Why?"

"I don't know." She paused, not wanting to harp, but at the same time, not wanting to have cigar stench as tonight's appetizer. "It's just that... Well, smoke ruins the palate."

He didn't move for a moment, then, straightening in his seat, he looked around the diner, taking in the glass-encased pie counter, the chipped oak tables, the soft truck-stop boogie from a corner jukebox.

A slow, sideswipe grin lit over his mouth. Even his eyes took on a devilish, I'm-about-to-zap-you glow. "People who come to places like this don't *have* palates."

"I do," she said, frosting him over with her best ice-princess glare.

He chuckled, jamming the cigar back into a jacket pocket.

At that moment, a waitress materialized, dressed in what could only be called "Matterhorn Couture." Knee-high socks shot out of tasseled loafers. Flowered suspenders held up a wrinkled, short brown skirt with a button-down shirt tucked into it. A name tag announced that their waitress was named Maxie, and Maxie's smile indicated that she was livid about her employer's choice of costume.

She posed with her pad and pencil. "Are you people ready?"

Rick gestured for Daisy to go first. It was about time for him to pull some manners out of his hat.

"Just a side salad, please," she said. "No dressing."

Maxie dutifully took this down, then tilted her head toward Rick while still writing. He ordered a Reuben sandwich, one of Daisy's favorites. She could almost taste the corned beef melting in her mouth, the kick of the rye bread. Ooooh, mercy.

After Maxie left, Rick appeared thoughtful. "You survive on that stuff?"

No. "Yes."

"Oh." A pause. "You really shouldn't dress in front of the window, you know."

If he would've leaned across the table and tweaked her nose, she would've been less shocked. "Excuse me?"

He frowned and shook his head. "There's no telling what kind of creeps are watching your window."

"Ah. Creeps like *you*." What had he seen when she was changing? Could she really have been that mindless? How humiliating.

"Right, Daisy. If you're going to St. Louis, you're going to have to pay attention. You can't be a little country girl skipping on down the sidewalks of the big bad city." He absently toyed with a table decoration, one of those Barbie-crochet fixtures that usually covered toilet paper in a guest bathroom.

He was right. Daisy knew it. But she wasn't about to feed his ego. "I can take care of myself."

"Oh, you can." He flicked a finger at the discarded menu. "You can't even eat right."

"That's what girls eat." Yeah, right, and that's how girls gained as much weight as she had over the years.

"What you need is a good meal, something to help you think straight." He called over the waitress and turned back to Daisy. "What do you really want?"

She wanted that Reuben he'd ordered, but she didn't have the guts to admit it.

He asked for another one anyway, as if reading her mind. When Maxie the waitress left, he fixed a hard glance on Daisy.

"If you need more money for food, just ask."

That hadn't actually been the issue. "I—"

"Don't argue. You're going to need a lot of cash in the city."

Something around the edges of her heart fluttered. She lowered her voice to an almost-whisper. "You talk as if you care, Rick Shane."

Silence. And more silence, until the food arrived.

Daisy ignored the salad and poked at the sandwich until Rick devoured his, giving her the green light to dig in. She was too hungry to simply watch.

As she inhaled a French fry, Rick grinned. Then she stopped, wondering if she looked like a complete garbage disposal in front of him.

She could almost hear him think, *So that's how she got so cherubic.*

Pushing back her plate, Daisy glanced away, afraid to guess at his opinion anymore.

His soft voice made her look up again. "I'll bet you never expected to fly into the sunset with Rocket Boy. Did you?"

Rocket Boy. A blast from the past. It'd been his nickname in grade school.

She remembered that much. When they were young, Rick used to take first place in the science rocket races every year. The teachers had crowed about his ability, but the other boys had started teasing him.

Rocket Boy, Rocket Boy, they'd chant.

And, then, there'd been no more science fairs for Rick, no more accolades.

"What happened?" she asked. "Everyone thought you'd work for NASA one day."

Rick leaned back, spanning his arms over the back of the booth like a pair of poised wings. He flitted a glance over her unfinished meal. Not much of a gesture, but somehow, Daisy found herself eating again.

The spotlight was on him, not her appetite.

"What happened? Let's see. Do you know what it's like being called Rocket Boy in middle school?"

"Can't say that I do," she said before chomping into the coleslaw.

"It was pure hell. At that age, you have no control over how other kids define you. I took control."

At this point, Daisy caught on to two things. One, that Rick had taken the attention off of her eating and was shouldering some of the mortification she'd been feeling. Two, that he was sitting there revealing something about his life. Something she could only now put together.

Everyone had underestimated this guy. Especially her.

She said, "Are you saying that it bothered you to be smart?"

He didn't answer.

"You didn't like the teasing, and so you cultivated another image?"

"It's not that simple," he said, glancing at her near-empty plate. When a slight grin crossed his face, she knew she'd been right about his intentions.

Who was this guy? Did anyone really know him?

Maxie cleared their plates, and Rick ordered two slices of apple pie and some coffee. Daisy didn't even protest. They were beyond that now.

When their desserts arrived, he pushed the pie plate a little closer.

"Gee whiz, Grandma, I'm eating," she said, anticipating his thoughts. "But I'm still trying to figure *you* out."

"I'm not real hard to figure." He took a bite of pie.

Right. "So you became Kane's Crossing's bad boy just to avoid wearing lab coats for the rest of your life?"

He chuffed. "It was more than just the Rocket Boy taunts. There was Lacey to consider."

Lacey, his stepsister? Come to think of it, there *had* been some kind of to-do years ago about Lacey. Daisy waited for him to continue.

"If you remember, Lacey had some trouble when she was a girl."

Daisy stared at him. "Lacey? But she's so lively, so—"

"Improved. She wasn't a happy kid. Real sensitive. She lived in a home for disturbed young women for a while but… Hell, there's a lot more to it than that."

Why wasn't she surprised?

He continued. "Suffice to say that I spent a lot of time defending Lacey."

Daisy ran her gaze over him, feeling sorry for the man with the crooked-arrow smile and the haunted eyes. "I'm getting it. You had so much to deal with."

He shrugged, backing away from the table. Joe Cool, once again. "The best way to stay out of trouble is to fade from the spotlight, you know? To be mediocre, to avoid comments and all the grief that comes along with being noticed."

A shadow swooped over his hard face. "So I started hanging out with the halfway crowd, the guys who could've given a fake nickel about getting good grades. All of a sudden, the pressure was off. I didn't feel the need to please the teachers, the other kids or even my old man."

Daisy remembered how the other students, when she'd been there, had gossiped about Rick flunking a year of school out of eighth grade.

"What did your parents think?" she asked.

His lips straightened, grimness weighing down the tips of his mouth. A mouth that had seemed so soft this afternoon. "My real mom had passed away by then. My stepmom couldn't have cared less. My dad..."

Was it her imagination or had his voice cracked? A fissure in the walls he'd constructed?

He continued. "I grew up a disappointment to the old man. But, at the time, it was something I could live with."

The words *at the time* all but echoed in the air, adding to the tense atmosphere.

Daisy sensed it was her moment to rescue Rick from a conversation that had become increasingly personal. "I think we have a lot in common," she said.

"Do we?" The old Rick was back, distanced, with that maddening glint of cool amusement in his gaze. She almost missed the guy who'd just been talking with her.

"Yeah. I've always felt a little isolated around people, too. This is pathetic, but do you know who my best friends as a kid were? Paper dolls."

He raised his brows. "Tell me you got rid of them before high school."

"Very funny." She tilted her head, remembering the tattered set of colorful companions she'd used to entertain herself while traveling from competition to competition. She'd made them work at Disneyland with each other, marry each other, have neighborhood barbecues.

She said, "I had only one good friend. But even that didn't last very long."

Even when she'd gotten older, post-paper doll

days, she'd been ostracized by the pageant community. That crowd had rejected her once the pounds had crept on to her body, making Daisy something they were afraid to become.

The entire experience made her wonder who her true friends really were.

She hadn't realized how much she'd leaned across the table, angling closer to Rick, until he glanced at her sweater. The one that had been smeared in apple pie filling.

"Points subtracted for lack of grace," she said, laughing.

Rick tried to smile, too, grateful for the release of tension. That conversation had gotten way too personal. But it'd been his fault. He'd led it in that direction, hating the way Daisy was picking at her food. It'd been obvious that she was embarrassed to eat in front of him. He knew this because she'd worn the same concentrated frown then as she had earlier in the night, when she'd jested about needing exercise.

How could she be making jokes like that?

As he watched her, he thought about how her recent shower had brought out a pink flush on her cheeks, more curl to her hair. She'd left it down tonight, and it was all Rick could do to refrain from digging his fingers into the mass of golden curls, to feel its thick comfort twining around his skin.

Rick made an effort to cool his gaze. He'd already given away too much about himself. Damn, why couldn't he have talked about the gaudy decor of this diner? Why couldn't he have talked about the weather?

No, instead he'd blabbed about Rocket Boy, about the agony he'd undergone as a kid who'd had to duck stones of gossip. He'd talked about Lacey, but luckily, he hadn't offered Daisy any details the people of Kane's Crossing didn't already know.

Rick needed to watch himself around her. In more ways than one.

As Maxie, the yodeling waitress, brought the check, Rick jerked it out of Daisy's sight without comment. When she started to protest, he merely held up a hand.

After paying the bill, he and Daisy walked back to her cottage, where he intended to drop her off before attacking his own bed.

They came to her door, which was lit by the soft glare of an old bulb.

''Thank you,'' she said, turning around to smile at him.

''No problem.'' He buried his hands in the pockets of his jacket, not moving an inch. He wanted to see Daisy safely inside, to make sure she didn't provide any more window dressing.

She stared up at him, her deep blue eyes shining. He didn't know what the big deal was. All he'd done was buy her a sandwich and subject her to stupid stories.

What he did know is that he'd never deserve a woman like Daisy Cox. A long time ago, after graduation, when he'd taken off for the Gulf War, he'd made sure he'd never deserve anything wonderful again.

Beauty queens like Daisy were lovely through and through. She'd never understand what he'd done to make himself so damned ugly inside.

She watched him for a moment, and he hoped his thoughts hadn't been telegraphed on his face. He'd worked awful hard to prevent the announcement of his feelings in that way. In fact, he'd worked hard to do away with feelings all together.

After a moment, she sighed, then unlocked her door. When she turned back around, she'd gotten all serious again.

"I mean it," she said. "Thank you for everything."

Then, out of the blue, she leaned up and planted a soft kiss on his mouth.

God, she smelled so pure, like a breeze combing over a grass field on a new spring day. And her lips were warm as they lingered on his.

Too quickly, she backed away, eyes trained on the ground as she entered her cottage.

Rick couldn't find the strength to leave. Not yet. Not while the glow of her kiss still covered him.

Then he realized that he probably didn't even deserve her thanks, because guys like Rick Shane never paid off their debt to the world.

He walked back to his room, feeling comfortable only when he hit the darkness and disappeared.

Later that night, Rick picked up the handset of the motel lobby's pay phone and dialed his sister-in-law's number.

As he listened to the sterile ring, he leaned against the Alpine-inspired wallpaper, noting the room's chintzy furnishings and fray-seamed carpet.

Before the answering machine on the other end of the line could respond, a male voice said, "Hello?"

Dammit. Matthew had answered. He'd been hoping to talk with Rachel, not his brother.

Rick's first instinct was to hang up on Matthew, but that wouldn't do any good. They'd done their rendition of hang-ups since Rick had left for the Gulf in the early nineties.

"Matthew, it's Rick."

His brother's full name sounded heavy on his tongue, especially since Matthew liked to be called Matt now. It all had something to do with the new lease on his post-amnesia life. "Matt" meant that he got to start over from scratch with Rachel and his family.

Unfortunately, Rick and Matthew hadn't gotten to the "Matt" stage yet. They hadn't really talked since the other man had returned to Kane's Crossing a month or two ago. Rick knew that his brother had regained all of his memories—even the family ones, the ones featuring their own past. He just wondered when he and Matthew would resolve their lifelong differences, because they had a hell of a lot to work out.

But not right now.

Matthew's voice lowered, as if spies were listening in on their phone call. "Did you guys get to St. Louis?"

"Nah. We ran into some bad weather, so we're grounded for the night in a place called Broken Wing, Illinois. We should arrive in the city tomorrow."

Matthew cursed, setting Rick on alert.

"What is it?"

Matthew said, "You know that Chloe Lister has been friendly with Rachel since she searched for me, right?"

Chloe Lister, the crackerjack private detective who'd found Matthew in Texas during his amnesia days. The hackles started to rise on Rick's neck.

"Don't tell me," he said. "Tarkin hired her to find Daisy."

"Right. Listen, you're not just going to leave the lady to fend for herself, are you?"

Damn, his brother. "What the hell do you think I am?"

A monster.

Yeah, he was. He'd done something years ago to make himself that way. And now his reputation was creeping out from the past.

"Rick, don't get pissed off at me. I'm just making sure Daisy will be safe. Chloe's good. Damned good."

The phone connection hissed as Rick gathered his composure. The last thing he wanted to do was allow years of hard feelings to come to a head during a long-distance call.

"I promised you all before I left," said Rick, his jaw muscles clenching. "I'm going to take care of Daisy."

The other end of the line was silent, probably because Matthew was surprised by the intensity of the oath.

Rick was slightly taken aback, as well.

But it all made sense. During his time in the Gulf, he'd been powerless to save Clarice, the woman he'd fallen in love with. She'd died while staring into his eyes.

Rick rubbed his eyelids, clutching the phone, trying to wipe away the image of his first love, wide-eyed and pale as the blood drained out of her skin.

He hadn't been able to save her.

"Rick?" asked Matthew, his voice sounding a million miles away.

"I'll check in tomorrow," he said, abruptly clicking off the connection and settling the handset in its cradle.

He leaned against the wall a second longer, a second in which he didn't even think he could walk.

Dammit, maybe he could make it up to Clarice, erasing all those sleepless nights that had tortured him with pictures of her face. He could make sure Daisy stayed safely in St. Louis, clear of danger.

She wasn't Clarice, but that didn't matter. Maybe he could get it right this time.

Rick walked back to his room, a new purpose in his stride as he thought of saving Daisy.

Chapter Five

The next day, after flying into St. Louis and securing a taxi to drive them to a hotel, Daisy couldn't take her gaze off of that Gateway Arch.

It dwarfed the city with a curved, gray shadow. Daisy even thought the landmark resembled a sturdy rainbow of sorts, and she was being chaperoned to the end of it.

The end of the rainbow. Freedom.

She turned to Rick, who sat next to her in the cab. He leaned an elbow against the window, the city's concrete high-rises and traffic-jam cars creeping by with bustling precision.

"You know," she said to him, "there are places that make you feel like they're a missing part of you."

"And St. Louis is one of those special locations."

His voice was as flat as a cold day, and it clashed with both the weather and her spirits. He'd been reserved—even more so than usual—since this morning, when they'd cleared out of Broken Wing at first light.

Was it because of his Rocket Boy musings? Or that little kiss she'd pressed on him last night?

"Yes," she said, determined not to let him ruin her euphoria. "I love this city. I love the Mississippi River, the jazz and the blues, the charm of a dark hole-in-the-wall where people can sing their hearts out while others listen...."

"Whoa, Sparky," he said, holding up his hands. "At least give me the chance to have a few of those hole-in-the-wall beers before you drown me in happiness."

Daisy huffed a sigh. "Can you be any more cranky?"

"Hell, yeah."

The taxi pulled up to their hotel's porte cochere, and a red-vested bellman opened Daisy's door, extending a gloved hand to help her out.

She shot a glance at Rick, just to see if he was paying attention to the definition of manners, but he was busy taking care of the cabdriver.

As car horns and the whine of protesting brakes echoed off the buildings, Daisy took a deep breath of the city air. No, make that city fumes.

Cough.

No matter. She still loved this place, especially

since this is where she'd start her new life. She'd already contacted Harry Redd about the hostessing job, and they'd rescheduled their meeting for later today. And she'd reconnect with her friend—and her apartment—next week when she returned from a business trip.

In the meantime, Daisy could hardly wait to walk along the riverfront, taking in the fishy smell of muddy water and the spirited calliope-whistle of tourist paddleboats.

Yes, everything was wonderful.

So why did she need to keep reminding herself of that?

Maybe because she'd deserted her sister? Her fiancé? Or maybe it was because she knew that once Rick left her she wouldn't have him to share the city with?

Rick had finished his business with the taxi driver. As he stood next to her, she was all too aware of his height, the power of his body.

"Ready to check in?" he asked.

Heck, yeah, she was ready.

As they walked into the hotel lobby, she smiled.

She was about to be reborn.

Late that afternoon, in his way-too-organized room, Rick sat on the edge of his king-size bed and shot the remote at the TV, not seeing a thing on the screen.

Click, click, click.

Damn, what a waste of time.

He shut off the television and stood, pacing until

he came to his window, which revealed a view of the ever-flowing streets. As he parted the curtains, he watched the faceless business people and tourists meander down the sidewalks, watched them go about their lives with definite purpose.

Well, he had a purpose now, didn't he? He was going to save Daisy Cox from her fiancé.

So, if he was such a hero, why couldn't he shake the guilt that cloaked him?

Maybe it was because he didn't want to worry Daisy by telling her about the private detective that Peter Tarkin had hired. Maybe it was because he hadn't been letting her know just how secretive they had to be in order to throw Chloe Lister off their trail.

When they'd checked in to separate rooms, Rick had taken care to register under his name, making arrangements to pay with cash. He only wished he'd been able to use a false name, but the hotel required ID.

Hell, maybe Chloe Lister wouldn't connect Rick's disappearance from Kane's Crossing with Daisy's own escape. Maybe no one in town would notice that he was gone. After all, it wasn't like he was a big part of the town's social scene anyway. Nope, he just spent his time flying his plane or hiding in that cabin by the woods.

No one would miss him.

A door next to his room slammed shut. Daisy's door.

If walls could talk, the after-shudder from that slam

would scream with frustration. It gave Rick a bad feeling about Daisy's return.

He ran a hand through his hair, waiting for her to call him, or to come over. It'd been hard enough letting her go to the Harry Redd interview on her own. She'd insisted, as a matter of fact. And he realized that he'd have to let her fly free every once in a while.

But not often. Not while the private detective was out there.

Besides, he'd spent the day constructively, inquiring discreetly about ways for Daisy to procure a new name. One that would throw Tarkin off her track.

Rick waited for a minute, arms crossed, wondering if he should swallow his damned pride and go to Daisy's room first. Just to see how she was.

Just to see her face again.

Yeah, forget that. He had no business looking at Daisy's face, or any other part of her body. He'd do his duty, then cut her loose, leaving him alone.

And that's how he liked it. Alone.

He heard her door wedge open. Then a *knock, knock* spurred him into a slow walk to answer the summons.

When he opened the door, his breath left him.

With her hair pulled back into a chaste bun, Daisy almost seemed demure. But not with those curves. Her prim blue business suit only emphasized her waist, the softness of her hips and breasts.

He clenched his hands, fighting the urge to reach out and peel off her layers, blue by blue.

Then he saw her sad eyes.

"What's wrong?" he asked, stepping aside to allow her into the room.

She took a shaky breath, dropping herself into a chair by the window. "What's right?"

This did not sound good. Compared to the bouncing-off-the-walls Daisy of early afternoon, this woman was downright maudlin.

"I hate St. Louis," she said, leaning her forehead in her palm and closing her eyes.

He didn't want to remind her of their cab ride, of her cute little, *Gee willikers, Rick, don't ya just love this place?*

Now wasn't the time for him to get her goat. Even someone as insensitive as Rick knew when to be a good listener.

He sat on the edge of the bed again. "I'm going to guess that things didn't go as well as you planned."

"Bingo." Another sigh. "I must be the stupidest Pollyanna on earth."

"Nah." Man, he wished he had a golden tongue, wished he knew how to relate to other people.

She sat bolt upright in her chair, thankfully unaware of Rick's inadequacy. "Harry Redd is just a dirty old geezer. I wouldn't have wasted my time if I knew that this *hostessing* job he offered was—"

Rick sat still, determined to be a help rather than a hindrance.

When she didn't say anything, he prompted her. "What?"

She blushed. "He wanted me to entertain his clients. And not by singing one of my talent songs."

Rick thought for a second, then her meaning hit him square in the gut. "I'm going to go over there and kick that guy's—"

"No, you're not, Rick. I mean, maybe I should be flattered. Maybe I could be the best high-class call girl in the country. Maybe I could win the crown for Satin Sheet Queen."

The image made his body heat up. "Daisy, you couldn't have known."

A golden curl had worked its way out of her bun, and Rick couldn't help thinking about running it over his lips, couldn't help wanting to reach over to loosen up her hairdo so all the spirals swirled over her shoulders.

Give it a rest, he thought.

Daisy leaned her head against the chair, watching him with that wide, vulnerable gaze. The kind of gaze that made a man want to shelter her in his arms.

"What am I going to do now?"

He shrugged. "You've got skills, right? St. Louis has job openings, I'm sure."

"What kind of skills do you mean?"

He just sat there. "Job skills, Daisy."

"You mean typing or computer programming or..." Her voice faded away as the first tear slipped from her eye.

"Oh, man," muttered Rick. Should he hug her? If he did, she might feel that unwelcome bulge in his jeans, and that'd *really* help. Or should he try some more talking?

Yeah, talking was safer. "What are you good at?"

She sniffed and stared at him. "Well, let's see. I excel at the art of mascara application. And I'm quite adept at both the inside wave and the outside wave. See…"

She flattened her hand and cupped it ever so slightly, using her wrist to pivot her hand back and forth. "Inside wave."

Then, with a more obvious stare of sarcasm, she moved her hand like a palm frond, back and forth, back and forth. "Outside wave. For parades, you know."

Rick grinned, thankful that the feisty Daisy from high school had returned. "Glad to see some of that spunk."

With a half smile, she sank down in her chair again.

"Hey," he said. "This isn't the end of the world. You said something about singing, right?"

She cocked her head. "There—the answer to my problems. I can sing for a living. Ha! Sure. Everyone's looking for their own private tweety bird."

"It was an idea, that's all."

"I know. I just thought…" She buried her face in her hands again. When she took a great, tear-jerked breath and peered up, her eyelashes were spiked with wetness. "I thought this would be easier. Boy, am I a dork."

"You are not."

That's it.

Rick stood, then helped Daisy to her feet. He closed her up in his arms, rubbing a hand down her back, nesting the other one in her hair, resting his cheek against her head until he closed his eyes, drunk with her scent.

Softly, he said, "I'm here to help you, Daisy."

The meltdown of his heart warmed his lower stomach to a temperature he hadn't endured in years. Maybe he could've even stood there forever, holding Daisy like this, enclosed by a bubble of stolen time.

A lock of her hair tickled his nose, and he shifted, moving his lips across the soft, blond strands.

She cuddled against him, her tears absorbed by his T-shirt, which had dampened considerably within the last minute. When she took a deep, cleansing breath, he breathed with her, their bodies reacting in harmony. Hell, even their hearts were beating in answering rhythms, playing tag beneath their skin.

He really should back away before one of them made the wrong move and things got serious. He told himself this a thousand times in what had to be an endless second.

But he wasn't moving.

Daisy's breath warmed his shirt, right over his heart, as she gave a tiny laugh. "Remember the prom?" she asked.

Sort of. He and some friends had flown the proverbial bird at the goody-goody celebration—it was called "It Must Have Been Love," named after that *Pretty Woman* song, of all things—and chosen to mock the tuxes and corsages with their own festivities outside Spencer High's gym. While couples had strolled in, with their baby-blue-lace dresses and teddy-bear dreams, he and several other disbelievers had serenaded their whisky flasks and hidden behind the bushes every time a teacher came by.

"Yeah, I recall a few things about the prom," he said.

"Do you remember dancing with me?"

Damn. He'd half hoped that the passage of years would've wiped that memory clean out of her thoughts.

"I'm sure you danced with a lot of guys that night," he said.

Daisy shook her head, rubbing her curls against Rick's mouth. He shut his eyes, trying to stay in control.

"No," she said. "It was one of the most boring times of my life. Tommy Bunch took me, even though we hardly knew each other. He hated dancing. So near the end, I sneaked outside to get away from everyone just sitting in the gym, staring at each other."

She didn't need to tell the rest of the story. Rick recalled every excruciating detail.

He and his buddies had been three-sheets-to-the-wind, big-time seniors, too good for stupid puppy love and cheesy dances. But when Daisy Cox had stepped outside, framed by a burst of blurred light bouncing off the basketball court, Rick had straightened up.

He'd whispered to his friends, "Here we go," and ambled over to Daisy.

He even remembered her gown, a jazzy red number, too sophisticated for the likes of those other high-school girls. Come to think of it, just today, Rick had seen such a dress in one of the boutiques downstairs, right off the hotel lobby.

She was a sight he'd never forgotten.

As he held her right now, he thought of how cocky he'd been in high school, interrupting her private moment and asking her to dance to the music that was escaping from the gym.

He'd expected her to give him one of those *off vermin!* glares she'd perfected, but she hadn't. Instead, she'd fixed a lonely gaze on him, and smiled.

They'd danced under the moonlight for a moment that was removed from time. A moment he'd never thought to share with her again.

But here they were, in each other's arms, dancing to the slow beat of memory.

Now, when she peeked up at him from beneath those tear-sharpened lashes, Rick wished he could go back to being that high-school kid. Wished he could correct the mistakes that had shaped his life ever since.

But he couldn't.

He froze, then stepped away from her, leaving Daisy with confusion written on her face in the stunned parting of her lips, the questions in her eyes.

After a moment, she recovered, crossing her arms

over her chest. "And now I remember how that dance ended."

"Right," said Rick, who'd darted halfway across the room to jerk his bomber jacket from the back of a chair and duck into it. "It ended with my friends telling me to get my Romeo rear end over to them."

"Then you did. Go back to them, I mean." Just like he'd gone back to whatever was stretching the distance between them now. Daisy wasn't sure what had caused the sudden tensing of his arms, the quick flight away from her. All she knew was that Rick didn't want her.

Actually, she couldn't blame him. She wouldn't want her, either. Not when she'd grown so unattractive over the years. Today's Daisy couldn't even hold a candle to the teenage Daisy.

Absently, she ran her fingertips over her hardly flat stomach. Reuben sandwich, French fries.

There was a time in her life when, after Coral had gone to sleep, Daisy would've eaten two sandwiches, a hot-fudge sundae, a bowl of cereal and a chocolate bar. Then she would've rushed to the bathroom, stared at the tiled walls while hoping to delay the inevitable, turned on the faucet that would mask what she was really doing, then…

God. Long ago, she'd been pretty enough on the outside. But, on the inside, where it counted, she'd been a mess.

Rick had stopped his desperate-to-get-away shuffling to stare at her.

Could he see through her? Was she wearing a banner that proclaimed Miss Bulimia, U.S.A.?

"You okay?" he asked, genuine concern in his tone.

She paused. "I am now."

After a second, he nodded.

"Where're you going?" she asked.

"To kick Harry Redd's face in."

What a one-track mind. "Don't you dare. I'm more offended than anything else. It's not worth your spending time in police custody."

He appeared to turn that over in his mind. "So then what do we do?"

"*We* don't do anything. I'll start looking in the newspaper tomorrow for job listings. That's a logical place to start."

He didn't say anything, just walked across the room to stand in front of her again. The scent of leather and brandy cigar smoke dizzied her.

"I'm glad this didn't get you too down, Daisy."

His leather jacket creaked as he lifted up a hand, flitting a fingertip over her nose. She couldn't help the smile that crossed her soul.

"Damn," he said, relaxing his stance. "In the meantime, if I can't go out and slam faces into walls, what else is there to do in St. Louis?"

The smile reached her mouth. "You're asking the right woman."

Rick grinned, too. "And I know just the right dress."

Chapter Six

That night, after having a meal flamed with Cajun spices and crisped-catfish pizzazz in the Soulard neighborhood, Rick and Daisy went in search of a hole-in-the-wall where they could hide from the world.

As they ambled, side by side, down a redbrick cobblestoned neighborhood where the ghostly wail of steamers floated off the gray Mississippi, Rick tugged at his collar. He hadn't worn anything as confining as a suit and tie since his army days in full-dress uniform, but he'd been compelled to snazz up his wardrobe tonight.

He chanced another glance at Daisy, making sure to preserve his air of careless appreciation. Letting her know how she was truly affecting him would be useless, dangerous.

He'd purchased that red dress from the lobby boutique, saying it was in anticipation of her finding a new job. The material shimmered in the mild river breeze, kissing against her curves, playing hide-and-seek beneath the sheer wrap she had draped over her arms. It was a dress made for nights laced with piano notes and low laughter, a dress that whispered promises before its owner was probably even aware of them.

She'd even done her hair up in one of those French twists, as she called it, allowing a curl or two to rub against her neck with the deliberate cadence of a man's thumb.

Ultimately, Rick had known that wearing his jeans, boots and bomber leather was completely out of the question.

Damn. He couldn't wait to get this dinner jacket off.

Daisy stopped in front of a place called Slim's. "I'm feeling the vibe from this joint."

The mournful song of a saxophone sailed around them, carried on the beckoning finger of aroma: the tang of baby-back ribs, deep-fried turkey, sweet potato pie and steamed collards all mixing together like the improvisational notes of a jazz combination.

When Rick opened the door for Daisy, the sax's volume rose. He couldn't help noting the flush on her cheeks, the gleam in her gaze. Together they entered Slim's.

The place looked like a refurbished nineteenth-century warehouse, with paint-chipped signs advertising steamboat cargoes such as cotton or tobacco covering the cranberry-dark walls. Slender dances of smoke hovered among the whisky-hued lighting, the burnt-ash floorboards, the compact stage crowded with musicians.

Rick and Daisy found a table near the center, and as soon as he pushed her chair in for her, he shed the damned jacket and loosened his tie, running his fingers through his hair for good measure.

Daisy smiled at him and leaned across the table. "Now *this* is paradise."

Then she settled back, and they ordered a mint julep and a beer, listening to the music of artists like Charlie Parker, Lester Young, Louis Armstrong.

All too soon, the musicians "took ten," leaving the sounds of clinking glasses and plates to take their place.

He tried not to stare too much at Daisy—what kind of red-blooded male could resist?—but she caught him one minute into the break.

Daisy's eyes widened, and she ran a finger around her mouth. "What? Is half my dinner still on my face?"

Look, but don't touch, thought Rick. "Don't worry."

"Then don't stare." She smiled and glanced away.

"Most of the guys in this room are peering at you, Daisy." And it was true. Rick had shot several hands-off glares during the last set. "I'm going to have to crack some heads if they don't lay off."

She didn't say anything.

"But then again," he said, just to fill the awkward silence, "you're probably used to men staring."

"No," she said. "I've been watched and judged since I was four years old. And I was never really comfortable, I guess."

"Four?" he asked. "How did your whole pageant thing even get started at that age?"

She fidgeted with the wrap around her shoulders. "Coral got the idea when people would walk up to us on the street and compliment me. She figured, 'Hey, we've really got something here, might as well take advantage of it.' Not that she was a con, or a bad person, you understand. It was a business decision, making the most of what nature gave us."

She seemed uncomfortable talking about her looks, and Rick couldn't understand it. He'd always been under the impression that beauty queens were confident about their appearances, had always thought that *they* thought they were too good for the rest of the peons. That's why he'd always given Daisy a hard time in school.

"You know," said Daisy, a melancholy smile curving her mouth, "I see pictures of those little pageant girls today, and I can't get over the unnaturalness of it. I looked the same way—like a fix-up doll. A child dressed in eye shadow, lipstick, mascara and grown-up hairdos. A five-year-old kid, just like I was, belting out *New York, New York* to bring down the house."

She paused, this time fiddling with the white tablecloth. "I only have one picture of me without makeup. It shows a normal kid in overalls with braids in her hair. And I'm smiling. Really smiling.''

Rick, as usual, hardly knew what to say to this. He had no experiences to match it, what with his cabin life. "I'm sorry," was all he could think to say without getting emotional.

"Nothing to be sorry about," she said. "It was a living, for a while, until Coral became ambitious about Miss America."

He sensed that she hadn't wanted it to go that far, but before he could pursue the topic, he noticed a zoot-suited African-American man standing by their table. Rick hadn't even known he was there.

Daisy seemed just as surprised as she greeted him.

The man shook Rick's hand. "I'm Slim. Welcome to my establishment."

Then he kissed Daisy's hand, lingering over her until Rick felt his face turn ruddy. The guy was looking for a wedding ring, the shyster.

"Miss, I couldn't help overhearing you saying something about singing."

Daisy almost sank down in her chair. "Oh, I didn't mean to…"

The man laughed, a sound like waves slapping against a paddlewheeler. "Don't be shy, honey. We all share and share alike at Slim's. Could you gift us with a song?"

"I don't—"

"Yeah, Daisy," said Rick, the old high-school tease creeping into his voice, "gift us with a song."

The challenge brought back *her* old spirit, as well,

and Rick's pulse soared. He couldn't stand to see her sad.

She stood, following Slim to the stage, meeting the returning band as she no doubt told them her choice of music.

Slim stepped up to the microphone. "Evenin', folks. Every once in a while, we here at Slim's have an angel drop into our midst. Now, you all know I've got some good ears, and when I overheard that Ms. Daisy Cox, here, was a songbird, I had to get her up onstage. Know what I mean? So here she is. Daisy?"

As the piano, bass, trumpet and rat-a-tat drums eased into a summer-night stroll beat, Daisy half sat on a stool, a microphone clutched in her hand, eyes shut.

Great, thought Rick. She's gonna kill me for prodding her to go up there.

But then, something wonderful happened.

She looked up, smiling at the audience under a sultry-browed invitation, and started singing an old Billie Holiday song, "They Can't Take That Away From Me."

Rick leaned back in his chair, watching the way she stroked her fingers over the microphone, listening to her husky voice teasing the crowd. She sounded as serene as a blues-tinged clarinet, floating its notes over the crackle of hazy candlelight. As she closed her eyes, absorbing the playfully sensuous interpretation of the tune, Rick knew he was a goner.

Maybe he shouldn't listen anymore. He was getting way too turned on by the way her red-tinted lips breathed into the mike, getting way too worked up by the way she'd started to look at him from the stage.

In a perfect world, she would've been singing to him, and only him. She would've been inviting him to slip his hands under that clinging red dress, starting from her ankles, rising over her calves, the back of her thighs...

Dammit. This was her act. Her talent.

It had nothing to do with him.

When the song closed, the audience applauded enthusiastically, but she refused another tune. Before she left the stage, Slim had a word with her.

Rick was going to get awful upset if the man was propositioning Daisy. He watched carefully.

She beamed on her way back to the table. "Hey," she said.

"Hey." Why was she acting as if she'd merely been primping in the rest room? She'd been seducing a whole room of people, for Pete's sake.

"That was..." He searched for the right words, knowing he didn't have a chance in hell of finding them.

She seemed to understand. "Thank you, Rick." She paused. "Slim wanted to know if I'd come back this week. Maybe sing a set or two with the band."

It was the closest thing to a legitimate job offer in St. Louis yet. "Good. That's real good, Daisy."

"Who knows?" She started moving to the new song, a little number with a jogging beat and bluesy rhythm.

She wanted to dance. He knew when that happened

with a girl. That's why he'd hated going to things like prom and bars during basic training. It was obvious when a woman was about to drag a man out there to make a fool of himself.

Rick slouched in his seat, trying to give off don't-even-think-I'm-interested signals.

When the tune ended, he gave a short sigh of relief. Until the band launched into the next song, a ditty that brought to mind hip grinding and discarded clothing.

Daisy laughed, watching him. "Are you in pain?"

Yeah, I'm about to have a damned heart attack just thinking about holding you.

He didn't react.

Daisy leaned closer, and he could smell her fresh shampoo even over the fried foods. "Know what? I don't have a fiancé anymore. How great is that?"

He glanced at her half-finished mint julep. "Is the booze affecting you?"

"Nope." She gave a little hop in her chair, cute as can be. "Let's dance."

Duh-duh-dum. The moment he'd been dreading. "I don't do dancing." He took the chance to settle the bill, slapping the money on the table with a "case closed" finality.

She rolled her eyes. "You danced with me at prom."

"That was different. I was young and stupid."

"Well," she said, "you're still one out of two."

As she laughed, he did his best to seem offended. "Young, I mean." Daisy gave him a lower-lipsticking-out pout. "It's not like I'm asking you to fly me to the moon."

Hell, that would've been a far easier request to deal with.

The band segued into a lazy song, and Rick knew that if he didn't want Daisy bugging him about shaking his groove thang all night, this was his chance to get it over with. The slow stuff was pretty easy.

He stood, reaching out a hand to her. With a "Yesss," she grabbed it, warming his skin.

Only two other couples were dancing when Rick and Daisy took a spot on the floor. With as little flourish as possible, he tucked her into his arms, and they moved to the beat.

Yeah, this wasn't bad at all. It was even nice, like that moonlight prom dance.

Except, now, Daisy had way more to press against him, with that slick material covering her breasts, making them slide back and forth over his chest. Even through his thin shirt he could feel her nipples harden.

Oh, damn. Now he had to deal with one of those escaped curls teasing his cheek, almost like a fingertip going "cu-che-coo, come here, boy, I've got something for you."

As she shifted, running her hands up his back and resting her head against his shoulder, Rick clenched his jaw. She had to know that she was chipping away at his self-restraint.

Don't be an idiot, he told himself. This is nothing but a slow dance. It doesn't mean you're engaged, it doesn't mean you're going to get yourself in trouble with a woman again.

But he couldn't help it.

Couldn't help imagining Daisy and himself as they faced a steam-shrouded mirror. Couldn't help picturing it as she leaned back her head in ecstasy while he eased off the red dress, inch by inch, watching it flutter down her skin to land in a pool of promise. Couldn't help wondering how her sweat-coated skin would feel as he slid his hands over her belly, up her ribs, over those breasts.

Oh, real nice, Rick. Congratulations.

You're the proud owner of a hard-on.

Man, how could he get out of this one?

She lifted and turned her head, propping her other cheek against his shoulder. Her warm breath whispered against his neck. "No wonder you gave me a *hard* time about dancing."

Hell, he could either pretend not to know what she was talking about, or he could recruit the bad-boy attitude to help him out here.

"Don't get so excited. A good girl like you wouldn't know the first thing about *dancing*."

Under his palms, he felt her back stiffen, and he wondered if he'd said the wrong words.

She poked a finger into his chest. "You'd be surprised about what I know." Then she trailed a nail down his chest, right down the middle, until she gave an emphatic closing scratch near his lower belly.

Other than tossing her over his shoulder and getting her into some misty corner to tear off that dress, Rick didn't know what to do. So he ignored the rush of blood to his extremities, trying to battle off the sensations.

"I'd be surprised if you knew anything," he said. "Don't beauty queens have chaperones to keep them chaste?"

She didn't say a word, and Rick took the chance to subtly blow out a breath of pent-up steam.

But he shouldn't have underestimated her. She stood on her toes, and aimed her words in his ear, tingling it. "I left my chaperones back in Kane's Crossing."

Then she took his lobe into her mouth, nipping at it, running her tongue around the shell of his ear.

He almost groaned with frustration, but instead, he stepped away from her, grabbing her hand, leading her through the jazz club's back door and into the neon-shrouded cobblestone alley.

As the cool air hit him, he gently pressed Daisy against the brick wall, raising up her hands over her head. Her wrap dangled from one arm in near surrender as her eyes widened.

He leaned in close to her. "What the hell are you doing?"

She gave a tiny moan, then rubbed her mouth against his. "I want you inside me."

Oooohhh, damn.

He promised himself he'd never get involved again. Clarice had hurt him too much last time, and he'd never recovered.

But...

"Daisy, you're making a huge mistake," he said, mouthing the words against her lips. Warm, so warm.

She traveled her hand over his belly, down to the pulsing stiffness between his legs, cupping it, using her thumb to rub against it.

She said, "Oh, it's huge all right. But don't tell me it's a mistake."

"You know I'm about to take you back to my room, don't you? You know what you're asking for?"

She leaned the length of her body against his, insinuating her hips against him. "I'm a big girl, and I do believe I know what I want."

He hesitated for only a moment, then led her out of the alley in the direction of their hotel.

What was she doing?

As Daisy waited for Rick to slide his key card in his door, she couldn't believe what was happening.

She was about to make some time with Rick Shane.

How many times had she fantasized about this during high school?

She'd always wondered about the pressure of his lips, how pliant they'd be, how they'd feel dragging down her neck. She'd always wanted to know the soft scratch of his callused hands as they stroked her waist.

Her bare waist.

Oh, boy. She'd been so jazzed about singing in front of an audience again that it had affected her emotions, making her adrenaline surge through her heart with the pulsing beat of a drum.

She'd wanted to celebrate her freedom.

That's right. She was single now, no longer an intended bride attached to a man who didn't really love her for who she was. She was free.

As Rick held open the door, she brushed by him, into his room. Light from the open draperies cast a whispery glow over the furniture.

Over the bed.

Yes, she was nuts.

And, on the dance floor tonight, when Rick had suggested that she was still "chaste," she'd iced-up, knowing that her goody-goody days were behind her.

Rick tossed his tie and jacket on the nearest chair, wandering toward the window, away from her. He seemed so solemn in the moonlight, not like the young high-school senior, arrogant enough to approach Daisy Cox on prom night. Now, he had an extra edge to him, a scraped vulnerability she couldn't quite put her finger on.

He came to stand in front of the window, a shadow with dark hair and eyes, with wide-shouldered apathy all combining, brick by brick, to form that wall around him.

She stepped closer, shedding her wrap on the chair by the bedside nightstand. "I'm not the good girl you seem to think I am."

He patted his hands over his chest, and she wondered if he was absently searching for a cigar that wasn't there. Maybe he thought if he could blow enough smoke between them, he could distance himself, let her down easy.

No. That couldn't be true. Back in the jazz club, he'd wanted her. There'd been physical evidence of that.

Why would he have changed his mind?

Rick glanced to the wall, showing his profile. A strong nose and chin, a corded throat with an Adam's apple she wanted to run her lips over.

He said, "I'll always see you as a good girl."

She laughed, wondering if he'd reject her when she told him the truth. "Well, I hope you don't have some kind of fantasy where you deflower the pure Miss Spencer County. A lot of guys have had similar thoughts."

Silence.

"Rick, remember when you mentioned the chaperone? Coral was mine. Through the years, as I lost control of my life, I did some bad things. Things I don't even talk about."

And wouldn't talk about to him. How could she ever describe the bulimia that had ruled her life for so many years? A time of self-hatred and secrecy.

"Daisy," he said, and she could see the slight smile on his profile, "I don't think you're capable of going wrong."

There was something in his voice. An aftershock, a slight quake. It made Daisy wonder what he'd been through in his life.

She took a deep breath, exhaled. "I got into enough

trouble to get me kicked out of the running for Miss America.''

''And what was that?''

''I…'' Just be honest, she told herself. ''Coral didn't allow me to date anyone. Except for prom, where she made Tommy Bunch promise he wouldn't lay a hand on me. I got tired of being ordered around, so one night, I ditched Coral and went out with a boy who'd been hanging around the pageant circuit.''

She'd been seventeen and in love. And she'd thought he felt the same.

Rick turned back to the window, and Daisy thought he might be angry, disappointed with her. Just like everyone else had been.

Though Coral had kept the liaison quiet, rumors had flown about Daisy and the boy, and that wasn't tolerated in her business. Gaining weight had only made the real truth easier to avoid.

''So you fell in love,'' said Rick, his voice unemotional. ''There're bigger crimes than that.''

And, from the way he said it, she knew he'd done something he wouldn't talk about, either.

She stepped up to his back, wrapping her arms around his waist, breathing in the scent of his skin. She ran her fingers upward, over his chest, feeling each defined stomach muscle jump under her touch.

In a throaty voice she might've used to sing a lazy, sinful tune, Daisy said, ''Please. Let's forget about everything right now.''

Rick groaned as she undid the first button of his shirt.

Chapter Seven

Only when, a moment later, Daisy had skimmed the shirt from Rick's body, did she notice the way his jaw muscles were twitching.

"Maybe I…" she said.

As she backed away, he grasped both wrists. "Don't leave, Daisy."

She couldn't see his face, but his deep, rough voice told her everything she needed to know.

He wanted her.

She leaned her forehead against his muscled back, feeling the sinew roping down from his shoulder blades. Feeling him take harsh breaths as if fending off the hunger of his jagged request.

Biting her lip, she moved one of her wrists. He had his fingers locked around it like a steel bracelet, holding her hand over his belly.

There was a line of fine hair trailing into the belt of his pants. Daisy used her fingertips to trace it, the downiness capturing her imagination.

She wanted to know what was down there, if he still wanted her as much as he had at the jazz club.

He spoke, his voice vibrating through his back, the muscles of his stomach. "Did it ever occur to you that I'm worse than anything this city—or Harry Redd—has to offer?"

She rubbed her lips over a shoulder blade, forming kisses into words. Valentine-hot stamps of desire. "You're not even on the same level as that man."

A second passed, maybe because he was allowing her words to sink in.

She asked, "Are you saying that being with you would make me no better than a call girl?"

He lowered his head, shaking it, and Daisy couldn't help freeing one of her hands to slide it over his ribs, up his back, his neck, to play with the longish-dark strands of hair, steam-curled from their contact.

"That's not what I meant," he said.

She rubbed the nape of his neck and whispered, "Would this be easier for you if I were a woman you didn't know? Could you open up to someone like that?"

A slight flare of hurt burned the edges of her question. But she couldn't help it. The thought of Rick with another woman made her want to scream.

A breath shuddered through him as he lifted his head and stared out the window. "I'm not what you need."

"Oh?" She pulled her hand away from his neck, cold air hitting her sensitive skin from the lack of contact. "And what do I need? Do you have any idea?"

When he didn't say anything, Daisy tucked her first thought to the back of her mind. Surely he wasn't holding her at arm's length because he couldn't stand the thought of making love to an overweight woman.

Could it be that he'd automatically responded to her playfulness earlier—like any man would have— yet his mind couldn't stand the thought of finishing what his body had started?

She moved away from him, misstepping, her high heel wobbling.

As if he sensed that she was about to fall, Rick spun away from the window, catching her around the waist, pressing her body against his.

He was so hard, with a broad chest that narrowed down to a chiseled waist. His ridged abdomen flushed against her, his arms wrapped around her as he bent her backward, blocking the outside light with his shadow.

It was all Daisy could to do to keep breathing. But when he leaned down and coaxed his lips over hers, she wasn't even sure she could manage that.

He tasted of their night together—soul food cooking, brandied smoke, the slight tang of imported beer. As he held her closer, his arms rubbed over the skin that her dress hadn't quite covered.

Bare skin, moist from the temperature they'd created in this room.

As he raised her up, his mouth still covering hers, she felt her hair slip out of its twist, covering them both with more silk and heat.

He nipped at her mouth, sucking her lower lip, using his tongue to slide along the edges. When she reached around him, pulling him closer to her, Rick swore softly, then plunged into her mouth, his tongue following the bluesy beat their bodies dictated.

They were both standing now, near to devouring each other, making up for all the years of wondering, longing.

He used his thumb to stroke the strap of her dress from her shoulder, and Daisy felt the slick material gaping, the air cooling her skin. Then, with a low, moaning buzz, he undid her side zipper.

Suddenly she was against him again, sans red dress, guarded only by a strapless bra, her lacy undies and a pair of red, high-heeled shoes.

Then it was just the undies and the shoes.

Rick bent to kiss her neck, to lightly scratch his teeth over the throbbing pulse of her vein. He ran his lips back up to her ear, heating it with his conversation. "I've wanted to see that dress on the floor all night."

She remembered how his own place looked, a cabin with jeans and T-shirts dropped carelessly on the floor. Hadn't the sight of them given *her* an electric thrill?

A gasp took the place of her possible comeback, as he palmed one of her breasts, teasing the tip of it with his thumb. Then, with deliberate hesitation, he kissed down her collarbone, her chest, and took her into his mouth.

She bit her lip again to keep from crying out. Instead, she pressed him to her, urging him on, shutting her eyes and running her hands through his thick hair.

While he swirled his tongue over the aroused tips of her breasts, Daisy lazily opened her eyes, half-seeing the steam-beaded window, half-hearing some partygoers stomping down the hall with their drunken voices and laughter.

She and Rick were...

Were they going to...

When would they...

"Yeah," she said, burying her face in his hair, scratching down his back with her nails.

As if spurred on by her voice, Rick lifted her up, spinning her around at the same time, guiding her to the top of the window-side table. As she pushed onto it, the thump of forgotten room service binders and tourist pamphlets hit the ground.

Daisy caught her breath, then wrapped her legs around his, taking care to avoid cutting into him with her heels. Their mouths met again, sucking, tonguing, exploring with frantic need, while he gently rocked her back, balancing her with his other arm, his fingers moving from her breasts, down the center of her stomach, over her belly, over her undies.

She was ready for him, and as he used a thumb to rub over the center of her, she cupped his hand with her own, increasing the pressure. She could feel the slickness of the friction, the burning intensity of blood pumping to the spot between her legs.

She wondered if he could possibly want her as much as she wanted him.

He peeled back the elastic of her undies, slipping his fingers inside, sliding between her folds. They kissed again, slower this time, moving with the rhythm of his touch. She pushed up from the table, arching toward him even more.

Rick drew his lips away from hers, nuzzling her neck, taking a second to breathe. Daisy made a sort of mewing sound, and it hit him full in the lower belly, sizzling there like embers being stoked into a new fire.

While he searched out the most sensitive part of her, he glanced up, recognizing a nighttime sky outside their hotel room.

He'd watched that sky earlier, when they'd first come into the room. When Daisy had smoothed against his back, her breasts pressing into his skin, making him even harder than he'd been at the jazz club.

In that sky, he'd seen the path he'd chosen to help Daisy escape. He'd seen the blue of her eyes when she got angry, darkening them to a murky shade.

He'd seen Clarice's gaze as the life had ebbed out of them.

Rick shut his eyes, lowering his head into Daisy's neck once again, hoping to get Clarice out of his mind. Hoping to get his past to the nearest dump site.

Daisy stirred against him, her leg brushing his

thigh. Her voice, breathy as the song she'd crooned in the jazz club, warmed his ear. "Whoever thought you'd turn out to be my hero?"

The last word snapped through him with the force of a truly aimed bullet. *Hero.*

He could've been one, before Clarice had died. But that's the last thing Rick Shane was.

A hero.

The comment froze him, the lost word burying itself into his gut.

By now, Daisy had obviously noticed the cooling of his ardor. He hated that he could make her look so sad.

As he backed away from her, the moon silvered her skin, her hair curled around her face, streaming over her shoulders. She leaned on her forearms, seemingly unaware of the way her full breasts were pebbled with desire. Seemingly unaware that she was dressed only in a pair of lacy red underwear and matching high-heeled shoes.

Hell and high water. Was he out of his mind to stop like this?

As she realized that he'd emotionally backed out of their lovemaking, she sat up, folding her arms over her chest. He straightened up, too, hardly believing that he'd put a stop to the fulfillment of his fantasies with Daisy.

"I'm sorry," she said, gaze trained on the bed.

Rick bent to retrieve his shirt from the floor. What the hell was she apologizing for? "Sorry for what?"

God, why couldn't he explain the reason he

couldn't go on? Not that it'd ever been a problem before. After Clarice, a woman who'd been everything to him but a real lover, he'd engaged in a lot of sex. Meaningless romps in protective one-night-stand territory.

Until Daisy, sex had never been a big deal. It'd been an escape, a way to avoid real relationships.

So why did it matter now?

He peered at the blue sky again. Why the hell did it matter?

Daisy alighted from the table, still keeping her arms over her chest. "I'm sorry for looking the way I do. I don't blame you for being turned off by my fat."

Fat?

What Rick saw was Marilyn Monroe purring at the camera in a haltered dress. What he saw was a museum-painted beauty languishing on a bed of rose petals. He saw curves, healthy, blushed skin.

No wonder she hadn't wanted to eat in front of him. And what had he done? He'd practically shoved the food down her throat. Idiot.

"Daisy," he said, trying to catch her eye. When that failed, he continued. "I never thought you were anything but beautiful."

Quiet. In the space of their tension, he picked up her dress and brought it to her.

As she slipped it over her head, denying him the sight of her body, she gave a stilted laugh. It didn't quite work.

"You don't have to lie to me, you know," she said.

"I gained a lot of weight after high school. You don't have to cover up your disgust anymore."

Was she thinking that he'd stopped making love to her because of her weight? Oh, damn.

He reached out, fingering one of her golden curls. "I don't know who told you that you were fat, but they were obviously blind. You're any man's dream."

Finally, she met his gaze. "Just not your dream. Right?"

He shook his head. "There's more to it than that."

"Daggonit, Rick." She shot her hands onto her hips. "There's always more to it. What's going on with you? Why can't you talk to me?"

What could he say to her?

She continued. "You started to be honest with me last night, when you mentioned Rocket Boy. Why can't you finish your story? If my appearance doesn't have anything to do with this thwarted attempt at seduction, then what is it?"

He cleared his throat, sensing a rise of emotion. When he'd vanquished it, he said, "All I want to do is keep you safe."

Would she understand his need to earn Daisy's respect, his need to make up for all the bad things he'd done in his life?

Daisy tossed up her hands in apparent frustration. "That doesn't explain anything, Rick."

"It doesn't concern you."

She glanced at the table, obviously referring to their passionate bout. "Really?"

Dammit. How could he get out of this without making Daisy feel like she was the one who had the problems?

"I—" He didn't know if he could do this.

Daisy moved over to him, running a hand over his arm.

"You can tell me," she said.

He shivered beneath her touch, not so much from the smoldering want of her—which was still raging through his body—but from the mortification he was going to feel when she rejected him. She was bound to feel ill when he told her everything about himself, about his self-disgust.

He thought for a moment, shutting his eyes to the moonlight.

In his mind, he saw his own once-upon-a-time, under the same moon on a different side of the world. A place buried by sand and greed, scrubbed to the bone by blood and the gnawing wheels of tanks.

When Rick graduated from high school, he hadn't taken long to celebrate. At his so-called party, he'd fought with his old man about taking responsibility for his life. Serrated words had been exchanged between them, and Rick had known, with all the conviction of the young, that he knew more than the ancient cruster. They'd had one of those arguments that can't really be mended; you never forgot what was said.

And Rick *hadn't* forgotten. Especially when his brother had taken the old man's side, busting out with a few accusations of his own.

Screw them, Rick had thought. He'd felt the overwhelming need to get out of Kane's Crossing, to fly in the face of everything his old man had ever believed in.

No talks of war in the Shane household. Peace, brother, peace.

So Rick had joined the army, needing direction, wanting a family.

Then Saddam had invaded Kuwait, and Rick's life changed forever. He hadn't really understood all the politics of the Gulf War. None of the soldiers he knew did. Most of them never even saw any action.

But he had, and that action killed Clarice, right in his arms.

He could still remember her blond hair, her blue eyes. She'd looked like a short-haired Daisy Cox to Rick, and that had been half of her appeal. That and her feisty temper.

There was also the fact that Clarice was an older woman, twenty-seven years on this earth. Divorced, but still pining away for an ex-husband.

She'd been a safe crush, Rick's first all-consuming Galahad desire. He was sure she'd suspected his feelings and probably thought it was real cute for a whelp like him to be trailing after her all the time. But she'd never led him on, never taken advantage of his crush.

He'd loved her above all else.

Even when they'd lounged around King's Five, waiting under the hundred-degree-plus heat to be trafficked to some action, she'd take the time to kid around with him.

"Why, hello, PFC," she'd say. "What is a no-hair

pup like you doing getting a suntan out here in the desert?''

Sometimes they could hear bombs going off in the distance, and a lot of the guys would stare at the action with patent longing. But not Rick. He'd stare that way at Clarice.

Until *that* day. The day he didn't like to remember, even though it repeated in his brain every night like a broken newsreel.

Rick opened his eyes, seeing Daisy standing before him. She'd obviously been watching his face, and he wondered if any of his memories had surfaced there.

As their gazes met, he recognized understanding, sympathetic willingness.

He opened his mouth to tell about the day that had changed him forever. But the stubborn words wouldn't come.

They'd already been deeply buried under shrapnel and agony.

Rick broke away from the touch of Daisy's hand on his arm, buttoning his shirt as he turned on a light. Artificial brightness blared over the room like an unforgiving sun.

Daisy stood in the same place, frozen with her hands balled into fists at her sides. Why couldn't he stop hurting her?

''Evidently,'' she said, ''no explanation of my repulsiveness is forthcoming.''

''I don't want to talk about it,'' he said.

Daisy bit her lip. She was doing her best to be compassionate, but she still suspected that Rick was dancing around the real reason for not making love with her.

He just didn't want her, and he was too polite to say it.

Nice time for his manners to show up, she thought.

"Well," she said, moving across the room to gather her wrap. "Thanks for tonight. Dinner was delicious. Dessert was humiliating."

He positioned himself in front of the door. "Don't be like this, Daisy. It's not you."

How many times could he say that until she believed it?

Heat stung her eyes, and she fought back the burn. "We're both running away from a lot of things, aren't we? And I'm not just talking about my wedding. There's something that's trying to catch up with you, and you're running for your life."

He flinched, as if he'd been slapped, and she knew she'd hit her mark.

"What if," she said, tears gathering, blurring her sight, spilling from her eyes, "we both just stopped?"

When he gazed at her, she'd never seen him appear so haunted. Even the irises of his eyes seemed like endless tunnels leading to one collective abyss.

She was going to try one more time. "Why do you hide in that cabin by the woods? Why won't you talk to me?"

Should she say that she'd even go back to Kane's Crossing if he'd come with her?

Would she?

Yes. Oh, God, yes she would. She might be able

to face everything feeling as she had in Rick's arms. There'd been a sense of protection, a sense that nothing could ever get to her with the way he made her emotions fly.

No, she didn't dare say these things.

Not when he'd already glanced away from her. Not when he'd already gritted his jaw, barring the words that might've swarmed around her, enlightening her.

Before Daisy could break into tears, she bolted past Rick.

And he let her go.

As his door shut behind her, old instincts came back to haunt her. Old discomfort and lack of control. Old voices, whispering temptation in the form of food that would fill her empty spots, in the form of a bathroom just waiting for her to run the water and cleanse herself of guilt.

As she opened her door, she headed for the room service menu.

Chapter Eight

The next morning, Daisy awakened still dressed in her red satin, with the room service menu clutched in one hand.

She squeezed shut her eyes, unwilling to greet the light pouring in through the gaping curtains. Slowly, she blinked open, noting that her digital clock read 7:00 a.m.

Why was she in this dress? Why...?

Oh.

Daisy pushed the menu off the bed. Her body tingled and her chafed cheeks heated up with the thought of Rick. They'd almost made love last night.

As she doffed the dress and showered, Daisy tried to feel some pride. She'd come back to the room hours ago, fully intending to return to her old ways.

To overload her senses with food, numbing the hurt, then...

No, she was over that phase of her life. Not even Rick's rejection was going to bring back the bingeing and purging she'd conquered in her mid-twenties. Sure, after the worst of it, she'd occasionally given in to pressure and reverted to those bulimic habits when the going got too tough, but those were only infrequent lapses. Daisy knew what the disorder did to a person: rotted their teeth, their insides.

She hadn't gone back to the behavior for over a year now. And even though she'd almost done so last night, she'd won.

As she donned her clothes, tweed pants and a sweater suitable enough for job hunting, Daisy tried to clear her mind of last night's physical activities. But she couldn't.

Oh, boy. What had come over her?

And what had come over him?

Daisy leaned against the wall connecting her room to Rick's, knowing that, on the other side of this barrier, he was there, running from something in his life, too.

Forget it, girl, she told herself. Because he isn't about to reveal anything to you.

To think, she'd actually thought about going back to Kane's Crossing with him. What a crock of romantic blather.

She straightened, going to the closet to slip on some flats, knowing that her feet were going to appreciate the break. She'd really given those red high-heels an adventure last night.

What was she going to say to Rick this morning? Would they avoid the whole subject, act like both of their bodies weren't pleasantly sore from the work-out?

Knowing Rick, yes. That's exactly how it was going to play out.

Heck, there was no use thinking about this anymore. It wouldn't get her a job. She needed a newspaper, a big cup of coffee and lots of positive thoughts to help her.

She walked toward the door, ready to start her new life and send Rick on his way out of the old one.

Her heart dropped to her stomach. That's not what she wanted at all. She kind of liked having Rick around.

To say the least.

Just as she was about to open the door, a shuffling sound in the hall caught her attention. Then voices.

Rick's voice.

Daisy peered out the peek hole, seeing a glass-warped view of the world. Not much help there.

But, just as she was about to abandon the spying game, two bodies came into view. Rick and someone else. A woman?

As Rick loomed over the smaller figure, he used a low, growly version of his voice. What was this? Anger?

Daisy couldn't stand it anymore. She cracked open her door, just a tad.

In the hall, Rick glared over his shoulder. "Shut that door."

Stunned at his hard attitude, Daisy hesitated, her pulse beating wildly in her throat.

A business-smooth female voice stopped her from going back into her room. "Ms. Cox, leave it open."

The woman ducked around Rick, but Daisy couldn't focus on her. All she could see was her savior, towering over the stranger with such rigid ire that Daisy wanted to slam the door before it was too late.

As she and Rick locked gazes, Daisy saw a mixture of disappointment and loss, not just dark anger. In his eyes, she saw nothing relating to last night—no reflection of the river's edge, no dancing musical notes.

God, she couldn't stand to see such bare emotion, especially from a man like Rick—a man who never let her know exactly what he was feeling. So she turned her attention to the stranger.

Silver-bullet eyes. Straight chestnut-colored hair sliced to the neck in a blunt cut and slicked behind her ears. Pointed chin with high, freckle-dusted cheeks. Garbed in a spiffy teal pantsuit, its creases sharp as the edges of the license she was holding in front of her with one hand. With the other, she held a tray of coffee and muffins.

"Ms. Cox," she said, "I'm Chloe Lister. May I come in?"

Daisy didn't even glance twice at the license, instead sorting through her mental files for the name. Chloe. Lister. Chloe Lister. Nothing seemed familiar.

Discomfort settled over her shoulders with the

weight of heavy hands. Hands like Peter Tarkin's, controlling and unwelcome.

Rick stepped forward before Daisy could slam the door. "Let's avoid taking care of business out here."

And with that, they both came inside Daisy's room, uninvited.

The first thing Rick had said to Chloe when he'd seen her marching down the hall with that coffee was, "Didn't think you'd get here so soon."

He'd been pacing the carpet in front of Daisy's room for a few minutes—okay, fifteen minutes—working up enough courage to apologize for last night.

He might've even told her why he hadn't been able to take advantage of her.

It'd been a sleepless few hours, catching him between wanting to be with Daisy and not wanting to tempt himself. Because he knew what would happen if he saw her again.

He'd make an ass of himself, spilling his guts to her, showing signs of weakness and pain—things he'd almost obliterated by keeping to himself all these years.

As Chloe had approached him, he'd shaken his head, fixing her with a thunderous evil eye. "Before I let my anger loose, I just want you to tell me why you took this job. I thought you were a family friend."

Chloe hadn't changed expression; she remained as efficient and unreadable as a corporate CEO. "That's the reason I accepted this assignment, Rick. Because I can manage things a random private investigator wouldn't dream of doing.''

''Like what?''

Chloe had taken a moment to check Daisy's room number, then—ice-sculpture-cool—had flicked out her license in order to observe proper P.I. etiquette. ''We'll talk about that once I see Ms. Cox, here.''

There was no intimidating this woman, but Rick couldn't help the rise of his protective urges. He'd cornered Chloe against the wall, minding the hot coffee.

His voice took on a soft, dangerous grind. ''Don't do this, Chloe. I know you've got a reputation to sustain. You're a businesswoman, after all. But don't talk Daisy into going back to Kane's Crossing.''

That's when his charge had cracked open her door, curious as always. He'd almost wanted to reprimand her for being so careless, but how could he do that when he'd been the one who neglected to mention Tarkin's P.I.?

He should've told her.

Everything.

Even through the tiny wedge in the door, he'd been able to see that she was still hurt from the way he'd avoided a connection last night.

But now, in her room, seated at a table that powerfully resembled the one they'd reclined on just hours ago, Rick tried to clear his thoughts.

He was going to get Daisy out of this mess.

Chloe had doled out the coffee and muffins, digging into the grub with relish. He and Daisy picked at their portions, avoiding eye contact.

The P.I. started with the basics. "Peter Tarkin hired me to find you, Ms. Cox, and he knows where I was headed."

"How?" asked Daisy. She'd cowered back into her chair, her light-brown sweater stretched over her bent knees.

All Rick wanted to do was hold her, but he told himself that was stupid. He'd had a lot of chances last night and, because of how he'd handled the intimacy, he'd blown it forever.

Chloe flicked a muffin crumb back onto the wrapping paper, keeping her eating area spit-spot. "Well, I have to say that Rick—" here, she nodded at him "—did a decent job of throwing some curve balls. But there was something, or someone, who doomed you all from the start."

For the first time since sitting down, Daisy and Rick locked gazes, both wondering, no doubt, what had messed them up so quickly. But after the first few seconds of common curiosity, their glances fell. Daisy watched the table, a mighty flush sweeping over her cheeks.

She was probably remembering the way he'd propped her on the table last night, leaning her back, making her a canvas for his hands, his mouth, his tongue.

Aw, dammit. He needed his mind here, not in a ruined fantasyland.

Rick tried to appear as casually unconcerned as

possible, stretching back into his seat, kicking up a boot on one knee. "What messed up our great escape?"

Her gray eyes sparkled for the briefest second, then dimmed. "Mrs. Spindlebund. She'd taken it as her civic duty to climb the church tower and survey any town activity. She saw a blanketed figure being huddled into your Jeep."

Rick grunted. He should've guessed that the gold medal winner in the Olympic gossip event would be his downfall.

Chloe continued. "And the rest is history. I checked into the Blue Grass flight plans and saw that you'd filed to go to St. Louis. Tracking you here wasn't really a problem."

A sinking sensation overcame Rick. Self-disgust. He hadn't been able to protect Daisy. He'd failed another woman, even when he'd promised to get it right this time.

Maybe Rick's dad had been right when he'd called his son a failure at the graduation party. Maybe Matthew had been correct when he'd seconded his father's opinion.

The truth hurt.

Chloe was talking again. "Mr. Tarkin still wants you home, Ms. Cox. I won't pretend that he wasn't livid about being stood up at the altar, but he's willing to forgive."

"But not forget," said Daisy.

Could Rick take Daisy to another town? The sudden idea jolted a rush of adrenaline through him. He could still get this right.

He said, "Tarkin laid hands on Daisy before the wedding. I don't want her anywhere near that man."

Both Chloe and Daisy watched him with surprise. Rick even thought he detected hope in Daisy's slight smile. But the emotion disappeared before he could be sure.

"Interesting," said Chloe. "To me, Mr. Tarkin seems apologetic, as if he's willing to let bygones be bygones. And, I have to say, I wouldn't be here if I thought he'd hurt Ms. Cox in any way."

Daisy put her feet on the floor, lifting her chin. "What would be the consequences of my return?"

Good God, was she thinking of going back to him?

Chloe said, "No consequences. He says he loves you."

Love. It was something he couldn't give to Daisy. Not in a million years.

Daisy sighed, shaking her head. "Things haven't changed. He'll call in that loan if I don't return, and that would leave Coral in a terrible position."

No, thought Rick, don't go back to your old way of thinking. You're worth more than a loan.

Then Daisy leaned back in her chair, staring at the ceiling with a wistful expression. "He's always going to find me. Isn't he, Chloe?"

The P.I. nodded. "And the next person who seeks you out probably won't let you know you've been found. You'll be running for as long as he wants you."

"Even longer," said Daisy. "There's pride and money at stake. Two things that Peter values above all else."

They were right. Could Rick take Daisy from city to city, always on the go from Peter Tarkin? Didn't she deserve more than that?

"So, Chloe," said Daisy, "what if I want to keep running? What would you tell Peter?"

The woman took a sip of coffee, pausing. "I think that, sometimes, you can't always catch up with your quarry."

Rick could feel the weight of Daisy's stare. He wondered what she was thinking, if she'd run with him for the rest of her life.

What had she said last night? Something along the lines of, "What if we both stopped?"

He couldn't stop, couldn't even think of facing his shortcomings. And if he stayed with Daisy, he'd break down, give into what she wanted.

She watched him, then softly said, "I'm not going to marry Tarkin."

His stomach flipped, but he couldn't tell whether the sensation came from happiness or fear at what she'd say next.

When he didn't answer, Daisy gave a sharp laugh. "Running any farther would be a big mistake, I suppose."

See. Last night had, at most, been a hapless diversion from what plagued her life. He couldn't believe he'd thought it was something more.

Testing her, he said, "Daisy, I promised my family

that I'd keep you safe, and that extends to Kane's Crossing. If you return, I'd make sure Tarkin didn't hurt you.''

All-consuming silence. She was probably thinking of how they'd kissed and caressed each other, thinking of how he'd never fully given himself to her.

When she spoke, her voice was as devastating as mortar fire. ''Don't worry about your promises, Rick. I can manage on my own.''

Her words carved into his skin, but he couldn't sacrifice his peace of mind. Not even for Daisy.

She addressed Chloe. ''I've got to stand up to my problems. That's the only way that makes sense, the only way to stop this ridiculous chase.''

Part of Rick admired what she wanted to do—face her demons head-on. Part of him wanted to spirit her away from every dark moment of life.

''So,'' said Chloe. ''We're going back to Kane's Crossing.''

Rick stood and walked out of the room before her soft, ''Yes,'' could twist his heart right out of his body.

''I'm going to march right up to Peter and explain everything,'' said Daisy a half hour later, tossing clothes into her suitcase.

As each article thumped into the luggage, Chloe straightened it, as if she couldn't stand any form of disorganization. ''If you have any trouble whatsoever let me know. But I'm sure he won't make good on his threat. He wouldn't dare.''

The Silhouette Reader Service™ — Here's how it works:

If offer card is missing write to: Silhouette Reader Service, 3010 Walden Ave., P.O. Box 1867, Buffalo, NY 14240-1867

NO POSTAGE
NECESSARY
IF MAILED
IN THE
UNITED STATES

BUSINESS REPLY MAIL
FIRST-CLASS MAIL   PERMIT NO. 717-003   BUFFALO, NY

POSTAGE WILL BE PAID BY ADDRESSEE

SILHOUETTE READER SERVICE
3010 WALDEN AVE
PO BOX 1867
BUFFALO NY 14240-9952

Play the Romance Crossword Game

and get...

2 FREE BOOKS

and a

FREE GIFT...

YOURS to KEEP!

Scratch Here!

← to reveal the hidden words.
Look below to see what you get.

Yes!

I have scratched off the gold areas. Please send me my **2 FREE BOOKS** and **FREE GIFT** for which I qualify. I understand that I am under no obligation to purchase any books as explained on the back of this card.

335 SDL DRTS	235 SDL DRT9

FIRST NAME   LAST NAME

ADDRESS

APT.#   CITY

STATE / PROV.   ZIP/POSTAL CODE

Visit us online at
www.eHarlequin.com

ROMANCE	MYSTERY	NOVEL	GIFT
You get **2 FREE BOOKS** PLUS a **FREE GIFT!**	You get **2 FREE BOOKS!**	You get **1 FREE BOOK!**	You get a **FREE MYSTERY GIFT!**

"Too many people know our business now, and maybe that'll keep him in check." Daisy paused, the red dress in hand. Then, with a decisive pitch, she threw it out of sight.

Chloe retrieved it and tucked it into the suitcase, then zipped the luggage shut. Daisy stared out the window. She was about to pass Go! without collecting any rewards. She was back to square one.

A tiny part of her had been waiting for Rick to say, "Don't leave, Daisy. I'll take care of everything." But he hadn't.

He'd just sat there, that explosive anger he'd exhibited in the hall vanquished to the back of his eyes.

It hurt that he wouldn't open up to her. Hurt that she wasn't important enough to merit an explanation for his suddenly frozen attentions.

Daisy laid a hand on the curtain, clutching it for support. Rick had only been tolerating her because of a promise to his family. He'd claimed no emotional stake in her escape. He'd merely taken what she'd offered—a slow dance and the need for the human touch.

She couldn't blame him.

Chloe broke into her thoughts. "Ready to go? We've got to head out for the airport."

Sure, she was ready. But what was Peter going to do when she got back?

Darn it, Daisy, she thought. You can handle whatever he has to give.

She turned to face Chloe. "I should say goodbye to Rick."

The P.I. bit down a grin, then said, "Maybe you should."

Daisy took a breath of fortitude, then left her room, heading next door to last night's den of iniquity.

He answered on the third knock, leaning his long body against the door frame. She took a moment to appreciate his physique—the boots, the lean-hard legs, the slim hips, the broad chest and shoulders.

One last look.

She tried to smile, but it strained over her mouth in sour-lemon agony. "I just wanted to thank you for everything. Even if things didn't work out as I'd hoped."

In more ways than one.

He nodded, his stare as intense and comfort-stealing as the end of the post-jazz-club festivities. "I'll be around Kane's Crossing if you need me."

No you won't, she thought. You'll be as unavailable as you were on that day I walked into the bakery with my wedding dress.

"I appreciate the concern," she said. "But I'm going to try to take care of this myself."

Chloe had come out of the room, bearing the suitcase. Rick glanced over at it, then back to Daisy.

Why did it seem like he wanted to say something else?

Daisy started to walk away. He'd had his chance, and now it was time to move on.

"Daisy?"

His low voice abraded all the self-control she thought she'd cultivated.

She turned around, tilting her head expectantly.

He straightened from his door-frame stance, as if he was going to wrap her in his arms and forbid her to leave. She wanted him to do it so badly she could almost feel his bare skin against her body again.

Instead, he merely held up his hand in a motionless wave. "Good luck," he said.

She couldn't move for a second, couldn't react, except for a stilted nod and a retreat in Chloe's direction. Then, with a small explosion, her trapped anger rammed through her common sense.

She whirled around to face him. "Rick?"

He was still standing there, watching her leave, face as indecipherable as shadows cast against an alley wall.

She ignored the lonely throb of her heart. "Look at me. I'm not running anymore." She laughed, actually proud of herself. "If I can do it, maybe you can, too."

Still expressionless.

At that moment, she knew he wouldn't stop fleeing from whatever was killing him inside. The realization stung.

Because, in her silly, sheltered ignorance, she'd fallen for Rick Shane and his secrets.

Without looking back, she brushed past Chloe, leaving Rick behind as she started on her way back to Kane's Crossing.

Chapter Nine

That night, Daisy stood at Peter Tarkin's wall-length parlor window, watching a sky that was slowly turning from peach-purple to utter darkness.

Her sister's voice chided her back to the moment, making Daisy feel like a puppy who'd wandered past its play area.

Bad girl.

"Daisy, the least you can do is face us," said Coral.

Reluctantly, she turned around, noting how Peter and Coral blended in with the crouched plants, polished antiques and stiff bronze-and-blue wallpaper stripes. Chloe Lister, who'd stayed behind to make sure Daisy was well taken care of, seemed incredibly out of place, not because of her appearance, but because of her discomfort.

Peter leaned against an aged player piano, coming off like a gentleman of leisure in a Noel Coward farce. Even after business hours, he was dressed to the nines with his gray pinstriped suit and tie, his black hair whisked back with expensive oils. Even the graying wisps at his temples demanded a certain respect.

He tapped the piano with manicured nails. "This is rather awkward. I never expected to scold my fiancée for the embarrassment of our botched wedding."

Daisy opened her mouth to tell him that the term *fiancée* didn't apply anymore, but Coral spoke first.

"Honey, I don't have to remind you that Peter chose to live in this small town because it's a family place. A down-home area where people care about each other."

And where the townsfolk knew everybody's business, thought Daisy.

Coral continued. "You were the one who approved our stay here, because you wanted to return to the town where you grew up."

Daisy almost interrupted again, wanting to emphasize that she hadn't actually grown up in Kane's Crossing. She'd just popped in every once in a while because of their pageant travel.

But Coral was still on one of her infamous, soapbox rolls, the permanent ruddiness of her cheeks spreading to her neck. That's what happened when her sister got going. Daisy wondered whether Coral would've become a walking red beacon if she had gotten her law degree and argued cases in front of juries.

She said, "Dizzy, we could've settled in Peter's Lexington house, you know. But Kane's Crossing appealed to you. And now you've really made it a hard place to live."

Peter even appeared to start speaking but Coral, still playing the frustrated lawyer wannabe, extended her speech just a tad further.

"This man has even taken us into his home as guests, allowing us to live in comfort. And you spit in his face."

Peter seemed amazed that Coral had finished, but Daisy beat him to the verbal punch. "I did no such thing. Can I remind the loving former groom that he slept with a bridesmaid?"

There. That quieted everyone down. Even Chloe looked mortified for Peter.

However, he recovered quickly. "Daisy, hon, it was just a bachelor party indiscretion. And, though it won't happen again, I hardly see the need to discuss this in front of others."

Oh, what a pig. He wouldn't do it again. Sure.

Thing was, she actually didn't care. He could roll in the mud with all the women he wanted, and she still wouldn't give a flying fig.

Coral left her position by a potted fern, coming across the room to hug Daisy. "Oh, my little Dizzy, I'm just happy the private investigator found you before you got hurt or..." Her voice lowered to a whisper. "I was worried, what with that Rick Shane's reputation and all."

As Coral stepped back to cup her younger sister's face, Daisy bit her lip. What she saw in front of her rattled her brain.

Coral, a sister seventeen years older and wiser, was a middle-aged mirror reflection of what Daisy might be like in the future. Blond hair that had faded to a dull yellow, eyes that had dimmed as if clouds were threading over a sky. Wrinkles punctuating all the struggles Coral had endured while raising Daisy.

She'd taken on so much to give Daisy a good life. The least a baby sister could do was pay some respect.

"I'm okay," said Daisy.

But deep inside, she was more than that. She'd come back from St. Louis knowing that a marriage compromise was out of the question. In fact, she'd even earned some strength during her time with Rick.

Rick.

Where was he now?

Daisy peered over her shoulder, out the endless window, wondering if he was flying the night sky at this moment.

Peter cleared his throat, and Daisy realized that he wasn't standing by the piano any longer. He'd come to rest right next to her, as if he wanted a hug, too.

Yeah, right.

She shot him an icy glare, one Rick might have applauded, and Peter stayed where he was, near enough so Daisy could smell his expensive cologne, far enough to keep her satisfied.

He said, "You'll want to see my newly acquired art in the gallery, Daisy. Familiarize yourself with them for the dinner party this weekend. I've got some racing associates who need that extra touch of attention."

He was assuming that she was going to slip right back into doormat mode. But, no. Not anymore. Daisy had thought that, after being fired from the last spokesmodeling job, she had no skills for any other kind of work. Yet the taste of St. Louis freedom she'd sampled told her that she could make it on her own if she tried.

It'd be so much better with Rick, but...

Don't even go there, she thought. You'll only succeed in depressing yourself even more.

Daisy met Peter's gaze, seeing paintings and race horses—the two areas that had amassed such wealth for him. "Peter, we need to talk," she said.

A thin smile weighed down his lips. "Certainly, but allow me to put things into perspective. Saturday, before the dinner party, the wedding planner will be stopping by. You'll also note the copies of the *Kane's Crossing Gazette* that are on the bureau in your room. There you'll find a few articles of interest, especially the ones detailing your sickness and how it affected your mood at the wedding."

"Sickness?" Daisy's voice was a croak. When she glanced at her older sister, Coral had closed her eyes, tightened her mouth.

Peter continued. "Before I retire tonight, I'll lay

these dreams into your head. You agreed to marry me in lieu of my calling in Coral's loan.''

He reached out, sliding a crooked finger under Daisy's chin. "I expect payment in full."

Daisy shuddered and jerked her head away from his touch. "I—"

He grabbed her chin, firmly positioning her ear toward his mouth. Then, he whispered, "I know you'd hate to see Coral in a waitressing outfit again. Or worse."

Cold fingers of dread plucked at her spine. Threatening *her* was one thing. But now he was after Coral.

As he backed away, a flash of light through the window made the gray hair at Peter's temples flare like Griffon's wings. "Another slip up like this will not be tolerated."

Then, smooth as snake oil, he left the room, nodding to Chloe in the corner. The P.I. watched Daisy, probably gauging the effect Peter's words had on her.

When he'd disappeared, Daisy flashed her classiest smile, trying to forget about his whispered intimidation, his harsh fingers against her skin. "That wasn't so bad."

Coral smoothed back a strand of Daisy's hair. The sensation took Daisy back a few years, to a time when she needed mothering. Wouldn't it be nice to fall back into that comfort zone?

But it wasn't possible. Not if she had any pride.

Coral said, "His ego is smarting, Dizzy. Don't take his hurt as a threat."

Daisy bit back a retort. Coral thought Peter was

God's gift, so what had she expected? For her older sister to change sides and support Daisy on this?

Chloe stood and walked over to the other women. "I won't leave until I know you're fine, Ms. Cox."

Was she fine?

Yes, she could handle this situation.

"Thank you, Chloe." Daisy addressed her words to the P.I., but looked at her sister. "Peter's not going to hurt me. I'll just be one of his pieces of art. You know, locked away and handled with care. Isn't that the life?"

Coral didn't respond, but her nose did redden, telling Daisy that she was gearing up for a speech.

It was definitely time to let Chloe go and for Daisy to fight her own battle.

Rick leaned against an elm tree in front of Peter Tarkin's glass house, hoping to catch a glimpse of Daisy.

Chloe had contacted him to announce their safe arrival, so after taking care of his Cessna, he'd secreted himself in Tarkin's yard, wanting to make sure Daisy was safe.

This morning's final words between them still slashed at his gut.

Look at me. I'm not running anymore, she'd said.

And he'd let her go, knowing that he couldn't stop his own private escape from problems. But in a moment of weakness, Rick had even toyed with the idea of blocking her return to Kane's Crossing at the airport, as she boarded her commercial flight home.

He'd talked himself out of it.

He'd do fine without Daisy Cox. That's right. Years had gone by without her being a part of his life, and there was no reason to go out of his way to add her to it.

So then why did he feel so empty all of a sudden? Why did the thought of going back to his warm cabin make him want to kick in a window?

Rick's gaze returned to Tarkin's home. People who live in glass houses, he thought, noting the strange construction.

Lithe steel beams provided a skeleton for the transparent walls. Beyond the fragile panes, inside the house, plants kept guard, offering only a glimpse of kingly furniture and cold walnut wood. Rick wondered what the back of the home looked like, wondered if that's where Daisy resided.

As it was, all he could see were those damned ferns and hothouse plants.

Or maybe she was in one of the extended house wings?

Those were the covered areas, more traditional with their brick facades. Daisy's bedroom was probably there.

Just as he was about to take a look-see at the structure's backyard, the front door opened, and Chloe Lister strolled out.

He waited until she got closer, then said in a low tone, "Hey."

She stopped, obviously surprised. "Well, aren't you the persistent one."

"I'm sure I don't know what you mean." Great. His feelings for Daisy were as clear as the house she was now living in.

"Don't play it cool with me. I saw how you two were moo-gazing at each other in St. Louis. You've fallen for that girl."

Rick shrugged into his bomber jacket even more. "You know, for a P.I. your detecting skills stink."

"Yeah, I suppose they do. And I suppose you're standing here—trespassing by the way—just to admire Peter Tarkin's architecture." Chloe waved a hand his way, dismissing him as she walked toward the car she'd parked on the lane.

As she passed, Rick asked, "How is she?"

Chloe paused. "Not in any danger, if that's what you're asking."

"Good." He settled back against the tree.

"Rick?" She came a foot closer. "Ms. Cox made a sound choice. Otherwise, this would be hanging over her head for the rest of her life. There was no avoiding the problem."

Yeah, Daisy had made a wonderful choice. She'd chosen a rich man over Rick Shane, a guy who couldn't give her anything beyond a night on the town.

Chloe cleared her throat. "She's not going to marry him. I believe her when she says that."

"And how do you know?"

She laughed. "Instincts."

When Rick chuffed, Chloe mock punched him in

the arm. "Don't get caught out here. This isn't exactly your fan club headquarters."

"I could use a good fight."

Rick felt Chloe aim one last stare at him, then leave. A short time later, in the near distance, her car roared to life, then traveled down the road.

He still didn't feel right about Daisy being here. So he crept with the shadows, to the backyard, near the brick wing, just to make sure Daisy was okay.

Daisy was in her room, finishing a phone call to her St. Louis acquaintance, apologizing for the false living-arrangement alarm, when Coral caught up to her.

It was colder in this area of the house, so Daisy had buttoned a cable-knit sweater over her other clothes, keeping out the chill. "Is there more that needs to be said?" she asked.

Coral paced the length of Daisy's guest room, making a blur of the cream-colored walls with their Monet copies hanging over the Chippendale furniture. Daisy thought it was significant that Peter's valuable art was stored in a secretive area other than the brick wing—a place where people could actually enjoy the work.

Her older sister stopped, spreading out her hands. "You're going to blow this, Dizzy."

Dizzy. Coral had given her the nickname when Daisy was too young to remember earning it—by spinning around to the music from her tape cassette until she fell on the floor giggling, too dizzy to walk.

"Blow what, Coral? We don't need Peter to have a life."

"What kind of life?" Her face flamed, making wrinkles stand out like readied whips. "You know I love you dearly, especially since you're so adamant about taking over the bread-winning duties in our family. But, Dizzy, ever since you lost that last spokesmodeling gig, we've been at a loss. How can we possibly pay back our loan to Tarkin? You didn't seem to have a problem with this arrangement before the wedding."

Actually, Daisy had nursed a huge problem with the scenario. But now, after knowing that she could be attractive, that she could possibly even sing for her supper, she had an even bigger issue with this situation.

"Did you realize," she said, sitting on her bed, "that people will pay to hear me warble away on stage?"

That night at Slim's wrapped her in memory, bringing back the lofty thrill of audience applause, the gleam in Rick's eyes as she'd come back to their table.

Shoot. Could she stop thinking about him for even a second?

Coral was looking at her as if she belonged in a straitjacket. "You're going to support us by singing? Oh, Dizzy."

"It's a possibility." Why did her voice sound like a tweet? Didn't she have faith in her own opinion?

Coral sat next to her on the bed, taking her hand.

"Singing was a nice talent for you when you competed, but it's a hard living. This—" she indicated the room "—is what we deserve. I mean, think of how Peter took us in when we couldn't find jobs. Think of the kindness he's shown with the loan."

Oh, he was a real keeper. He'd made her feel especially valued when he'd slept with Liza Cochrane.

"You don't understand," said Daisy, growing wearier by the moment.

Coral adapted her patient sister-knows-best voice. "I don't? I see a man who's crazy about you. A man who'll treat you well for the rest of your life. So he had a little slipup. That's a guy for you. And it happened before the wedding."

"You're justifying his behavior?"

"Of course not."

Daisy thought something snapped across Coral's eyes. Something like regret.

Her sister said, "I quit college and let a promising law career flap in the wind to give you the life you deserved. This is our reward for your pageant work— my pulling double shifts at all those waitressing gigs? Back then, when we had sponsors who didn't come through, or when you didn't quite win enough money for us to make it to the next month, I used to tell myself that there was a pot of gold at the end of the rainbow. That fate wouldn't give us such a hard life unless we'd be rewarded in the future."

Coral placed a hand on Daisy's shoulder. "This is our just dessert."

True. Coral had earned the good life for taking care

of Daisy all those years, for sacrificing her own career for Daisy's.

Maybe her time with Rick had been a mirage. A fleeting glimpse into a fantasy, complete with smoky jazz clubs and burning caresses.

Her time with him was gone. He'd made sure of it.

Maybe this was how life would be for her. It'd probably been predetermined, along with the day the world would end.

She sighed. This would be so much easier if she hadn't thought a change was possible with Rick.

Coral stood. "I'll leave you to your thoughts, Dizzy. I love you."

"Love you, too." Daisy tried to smile as Coral left the room.

Her sister had spent years proving her love to Daisy. Rick had been in her life for less than a week.

As she got up from the bed, Daisy shed her sweater. Then, remembering how Rick had been so concerned about her dressing in front of windows, she moved to the curtains, intending to shut them.

For a second she paused, watching the glow of distant Main Street's lights spraying upward into the sky.

She wasn't a doormat.

She was going to think of a way to pay off that loan. A way to tell Peter that she wouldn't marry him. A way to avoid disappointing her sister.

So much to think about.

She sighed again, stirring the sheer curtains as she started to pull them shut.

Then she saw something, by the bushes. A flash of brown, disappearing as quickly as the flick of a lighter.

For a beautiful second, she thought Rick was coming to storm this fortress, that he was playing knight to her lady in distress.

Wow, was she a dork.

Rick was probably locked away in his cabin, content to be all by himself for the rest of his miserable life.

And with that final thought, she snapped shut the curtains, obliterating the night.

Chapter Ten

That Saturday the Cutter's Lake Shopping Arcade, built by Nick Cassidy on a pier resplendent with rainbow-hued balloons, ragtime music and wind-faded gray wood, was choked with kids wanting to ride the carousel.

Rick's niece, Tamela, was one of the Merry-Go-Round's biggest fans. From her seat on a pink-and-white horse she called "Candy Cane," the little girl waved to him and her father, Matthew. Every once in a while, his sister-in-law Rachel would flash by, hand on her slightly rounded tummy while seated on a gem-encrusted seat, watching Tamela ride to the calliope music.

Matthew hated the contraption. Wouldn't go near it. And Rick didn't exactly feel manly about standing among the pastel horses and flash-bulb mirrors.

So, that left them here, slouching on opposite ends of a green bench, waiting for Tamela to finish her marathon.

Matthew tilted back his ever-present cowboy hat. "Three rides and counting. One day Tamela conquered this thing twelve times."

"It's better than her playing mind-sapping video games, I suppose," said Rick, stifling a yawn.

He'd finally made his way to the cabin last night after staring at Daisy's bedroom window for hours. After she'd zinged shut her curtains earlier in the evening, he'd stuck around, hoping Tarkin would behave himself. At the same time, he'd also hoped that she'd catch him out by the bushes.

There'd been a second when she'd paused, staring his way. Soft lamplight had haloed her curls, had made her figure into an hourglass that reminded him of each moment they'd spent together.

Each wasted moment.

As the carousel stopped, Tamela and Rachel stayed on, causing Matthew to huff out a sigh.

He said, "You've gotta be happy that you chose to hang out with the family today."

The way Matthew said the words, they almost sounded accusatory. Almost as if he preferred that Rachel hadn't invited Rick to come along. And he almost hadn't, dreading the disappointment his family was bound to feel at his failure with Daisy's escape.

But Rachel and Matthew had surprised him, merely telling him that he'd tried his best and that's what counted. That they were proud of his willingness to help.

The last comment had shocked Rick right out of his boots. Matthew hadn't really ever complimented him before this whole fiasco.

Damn, they'd been uncomfortable around each other for years. Rick had even thought—hoped—that when his brother had conquered amnesia and changed his life from the playboy he used to be to the stable father and husband he was now, that he'd include Rick in his mental makeover.

No such luck.

They just couldn't talk with each other, not since their middle-school days, when Matthew had broken ahead in the race for their father's approval.

Rick had given up once Matthew had started bringing home perfect grades and sports letters for his school jacket. He'd gladly provided the family with a screwup.

Only too late had he realized that being the black sheep wasn't as fulfilling as being the favored son.

Matthew leaned forward on the bench, watching Rick. "At least Tamela's going to buy us some time together."

Rick froze. Maybe this was it—the moment his wounded feelings would be exposed.

He'd lost Daisy because of his inability to face the past. Maybe, with Matthew, he should think about staring down old problems, solving them.

"We haven't really been friendly for a while," said Rick, testing his sibling.

"Yeah." Matthew stared straight ahead, but Rick knew he was listening, giving him his full attention.

"I don't know what's in your head," he said, leaning forward as well. "I haven't been sure about which memories you got back, which ones are still gone."

"Hell. I don't have a checklist. But I do remember saying things to you that I regret."

Rick's graduation day. It was on both their minds, spoken or not.

When Rick didn't say anything, Matthew continued. "I started getting too big for my britches around that time, thought I could be Dad. I even took his side on things just to feel his power, I think."

"You're lucky you didn't expire of a bad ticker, too." His dad's death still lived in Rick's own heart, chipping away at him every day because he'd never been able to apologize for leaving, for never making the effort to talk with him again.

Matthew clasped his hands, his stare on the wooden-plank floor. The sweet stench of cotton candy clutched at Rick's stomach as he waited for his brother to pierce him with more almost-apologies.

Matthew said, "I had no business eavesdropping on you and Dad on graduation day. I'd already started college though, and that meant I was an adult. When I got tired of drinking punch and chatting with relatives over cake, I wandered around, hearing voices in Dad's study."

Rick closed his eyes, still stupid enough to allow his father's ghostly opinions to matter. "You're an embarrassment to the Shane name," his dad had said, brown eyes bulging, veins popping. Even back then, Rick had known his old man was in for a heart attack.

Then he'd piled on more hurt. "I'm not spending a dime on a higher education for a layabout like you. You'd flunk out of college the first week."

In the midst of this, Matthew had strolled in with his favorite-son haircut and grin, his smug confidence echoing their father's. When Rick had started defending himself—he had a brain, dammit, he used to be able to make rockets that flew from one end of the playground to the other—it'd been years too late. He'd already convinced everyone that he was a waste of classroom time, a bad investment.

He'd felt so helpless that he'd said something he knew would make his father suffer. "Well, if you're gonna be so stubborn with your money, I'm gonna take care of myself. The army can give me an education." The army could teach him how to fly again.

His anti-military father had blanched, but Matthew had taken up the slack at that point.

"Maybe the army will make a man out of you, Rick. Don't come back until that happens."

The words had stunned Rick, ringing in his ears even as he stubbornly enlisted with the local recruiters that same day.

Yeah, he had become a man all right. Matthew would never know just how much Rick had paid with his soul to cash in on the title.

Rick blinked, realizing that Matthew was still talking.

"I can't apologize enough for that day." His

brother turned his head, meeting Rick's gaze head-on. "I don't know how to erase what I said, what Dad said, but I'm going to do my damnedest to try."

Rick nodded, not trusting himself to speak.

Matthew reached over, thumping Rick's back. "There aren't many men who'd drop their lives to save a woman they hardly knew. You're the best of the lot, Rick, and you make me envy your sense of honor."

"I messed it up." Even now, he couldn't stop beating on himself.

"You did your best, and there's not a person who matters who doesn't admire the hell out of you."

Most brothers would've hugged or perhaps made an attempt at affection. Rick didn't know if he and Matthew were quite there yet, but he had the feeling that, maybe in the future, they'd be able to further mend their fences.

"Thanks, Matthew," he said.

"One more thing." His brother grinned. "I go by Matt now."

Rick nodded. They'd crossed to the "Matt" phase, just like Rachel had.

As the makings of a smile started to cross his mouth, Rick lifted his head, halting all signs of happiness.

Daisy stood by the gates of the carousel, sunburst mirrors catching the light of her hair. She wore a copper blazer that hugged her waist, complemented by matching pants and shoes. Polished as a new penny.

She'd also draped a multicolored scarf over one shoulder, adding typical finesse to her appearance.

As she clutched her purse in front of her, Matthew—no, Matt—cleared his throat.

"Ricky," he said, "I think you have some 'splaining to do."

Rick stood, and walked over to her, pretending—even to himself—that it didn't matter.

Daisy turned to the carousel when Rick rose from the bench. She hadn't meant to interrupt the intense conversation between him and his brother, but she'd done it anyway, unintentionally.

Wasn't she always butting into his life?

She watched Rachel on the merry-go-round. The woman couldn't take her eyes off her daughter. It almost stung to see such a happy family.

Daisy wasn't sure it'd ever happen to her. The family. Love and true affection. And, the thing was that right now, staring at mother and daughter laughing together, she wanted a child and a husband who truly loved her more than anything.

Rick shuffled next to her, hands stuffed into his bomber jacket pockets. "Fancy seeing you here. Where's the hubby?"

God, that smarted, almost as much as the prickles of desire that were biting her skin. Almost as much as the nervous twisting heat in her belly. "Let me correct your take on current events. I'm not married, remember?"

"Not yet."

"Listen," she said, exhaling with frustration. "I'm not here to pick a fight with you. All I wanted was to get out of that house. I even ditched the wedding planner, heaven forbid."

He grinned, looking impressed with her. "Yeah? You're a sneaky one, Daisy."

"What a newsflash."

Rick's voice lowered. "Is it that bad, staying there?"

No, it wasn't bad. It was just...

Wrong.

"If you enjoy big sisters who constantly remind you that they know what's best for you, then yes, it is bad. Otherwise, I'm just fine."

"So who's planning the wedding? Don't you at least want a say in the menu?" Rick patted down his jacket, pulling a cigar from its depths.

Funny how that stick of death kept him occupied when he most needed it. She said, "I'm going to start wearing a sign that claims, I'm Not Marrying Peter Tarkin."

"You're living in his house."

True. And the fact had bothered her more than she wanted to admit. She'd have to make arrangements to move out as soon as possible.

When she didn't answer, Rick started ambling away. Then, when he noticed she wasn't following, he nodded his head toward the exit.

"Come on," he said.

She followed, out into the lake-ruffled breeze, past

hot-dog carts and fishermen, down the pier until they reached the end.

As he lit his cigar and took a puff, Rick kept his eyes on the lake, even going so far as to pick up a stray stick of wood from a nearby pine and skip it over the surface.

She couldn't stand the silence. "You've got the cutest little niece. She rides that carousel pony like it's galloping on the clouds."

"Yup, that's Tamela, princess in the making."

She paused. "I wonder what it's like to be able to spend a Saturday afternoon with parents, laughing with them."

He picked up another piece of wood and absently ran his finger over it, watching her. His dark eyes held a million questions. "You never had fun with Coral?"

"Not really. I had to stay out of the sun, because it'd damage my skin, so we never had picnics or went to the park. I wasn't allowed to play with the other kids in our neighborhood because I might scrape my knee or get hurt."

Daisy smiled. "But I did have a friend once, when I was six. I went over to her house, and we played 'haircut.' She chopped my bangs so short that I started to cry. I remember saying, 'I look like a brat!' Whatever that means."

Rick chuckled. "And when you got home?"

"Coral was fit to be tied. I never saw that little girl again. Her name was Becky." Another hesitation. "I remember because she was the only friend I really ever had. Not until after the pageants.''

He puffed on the cigar. ''It hurts to see you, Daisy.''

She froze, hardly believing what he'd just said.

A full minute passed, one in which Rick busied himself by tossing another stick into the lake, the object skipping over the water with a glee Daisy coveted.

Finally, he spoke again. ''I hate that look in your eyes. It's almost a plea, and I don't know what to do about it.''

''A plea for what?'' Had she been reduced to silently begging for his touch again? Was she that transparent?

He paused, then wheeled around to face her. ''I don't want to rehash everything.''

''You brought it up.''

He clenched his free fist, longing apparent in the way he moved a step nearer, in the way he watched her.

The emotion reflected her own. Their time in St. Louis washed over her, drowning her in the feel of his bare chest pressed against hers, his lips trailing down her body in a line of lazy fire.

How would Peter have reacted to seeing her in that most vulnerable state?

She had the notion that her former fiancé would've turned up his nose and asked her when she would start her next diet.

Just like he had this morning, when she'd come

downstairs for breakfast. He'd already had her meal waiting, a soft-boiled egg surrounded by fresh fruit and vegetables. Everyone else had been served eggs Benedict, so Daisy had received the hint loud and clear.

Not that she didn't want to shave off a few pounds. But she wanted to do it in her own time. Having someone else structure her eating habits merely added to her sense of being locked away in a gilded cage.

As Rick moved closer to her, his other hand reaching out to touch her cheek, Daisy shook her head.

"Damn you, Rick Shane."

He stopped. "What...?"

She rolled her eyes. "Why'd you have to go and be so nice to me? Why'd you have to tell me that I was beautiful that night in St. Louis?"

"Because you are."

"No! See..." She drew in a shaky breath, then let it go. "You're not playing fair. Now you're going to make me expect such compliments from every man I meet."

He closed his eyes, running a hand through his hair. When he opened them, his gaze had cooled to confusion more than anything else. "You're Miss Spencer County. Haven't you been complimented all your life?"

"It's not the same." How could she explain that pretty words meant more now that she was many pounds beyond the crown?

She continued. "And would you just forget about the whole beauty-queen thing?"

His mouth quirked into a crooked grin before he took another draw on his cigar, leisurely blowing out a cloud of smoke. "Only if you can."

She sniffed. Wow. She really had been using her title a lot lately. She'd been wielding it like a spiked mace, daring Rick to duck its challenge.

Tossing up her hands, she gave up. "All right. I hereby throw all past-life references out the window."

From the way his jaw tightened, Daisy thought that Rick had done the same long ago. In fact, she knew it was true. That's why he hadn't been able to give his all to her the other night.

"You don't have to go that far," he said. "Those experiences make you the woman you are today. And I kinda like that woman."

Daisy felt as if the sun had broken free of its chains and was bursting all over the sky. "I guess I like you, too."

No use telling him how she really felt. That she actually might have gone and fallen in love with him already.

They stood on the pier like two awkward kids, golly-geeing as a boat with two fishermen floated by.

When she next glanced at him, he'd somehow moved closer. Stealthy fellow.

She caught her breath, telling herself to control her heartbeat. Of course, it was crazy to tell herself things like that. She had no control over her instincts. Over her body. Over her feelings for Rick.

He slipped a hand behind her neck, massaging her

skin. Her eyes drifted closed, lulled by the warmth of his fingers.

Then, just as quickly, she opened her eyelids. "Not here, Rick."

Not now. Not anytime, actually. This was the guy who'd all but dumped her the other night. What was she doing, allowing him to touch her like this?

Even if the burn of his fingertips flowed down her neck, through her spinal cord and all over her belly, she still couldn't let him hurt her again.

"Not here?" he asked, removing his hand. "Are you afraid someone's going to see? Maybe Mrs. Spindlebund is spying on us, getting ready to tattle to Tarkin."

How could she explain her confusion, her need to have more than an insignificant fling? She'd dated more than just the boy who'd led her to heartbreak at seventeen years of age. But she'd never kissed someone as passionately as she had Rick, never allowed anyone to swerve so near the emptiness of her heart.

She backed away, tucking her purse under her arm. "I've got to buy flower arrangements for a dinner party tonight."

Peter's going to wonder where I've been.

No. That wasn't it at all. It was simply an excuse to stay away from Rick Shane.

"Daisy?"

She stopped, wondering if she wanted to hear anything more that he had to say.

He worked the last of his cigar, seemingly unconcerned about her most recent escape. "If you ever need me, day or night, you know where I am."

Touched, she pressed her fingers to her throat, soothing the emotional burn there. He had no idea how much those words meant to her.

Before she could thank him, he raised a hand and glanced back at the lake before he wandered farther down the pier.

As Daisy watched him go, she pinched her thigh, punishing herself, maybe even trying to wake herself up.

Only when Rick had become a blurred shape against the sun did she turn around to leave, regret making every step toward tying up her loose ends that much harder.

Chapter Eleven

The Saturday dinner party had been an utter disaster.

As Daisy strolled through Peter's art gallery the next night, admiring more new acquisitions, she tried to forget about the tasteless Steak Diane, the stilted table conversation that she hadn't been able to rescue.

She'd been too affected by seeing Rick at the shopping arcade, too swept away by the hungry roll of blood under her skin.

Peter had expressed his disappointment after the party, but Daisy hadn't heard a word. As she'd watched his mouth work around his complaints, she merely told herself that she was doing the right thing by gradually attempting to fade out of Peter's life.

He wasn't even catching onto the subtle hints she'd been making: spacing out during his conversations with her, packing small boxes of her belongings in readiness to move out of Peter's residence.

Rick's stepsister, Lacey Vedae, had invited Daisy to use one of the bedrooms at her home, and Daisy had accepted, but only on the condition that it was temporary. Starting tomorrow, she would find a job and start paying off Peter's loan again.

Coral couldn't talk her out of it this time. Even if Daisy had to work her fingers to the bone every day for the rest of her life, she'd be her own person—not Peter's trophy.

In the meantime, she'd find a place for her and Coral, even though she didn't expect her sister to be entirely cooperative in this endeavor.

So, on this, her last night as Peter's guest, Daisy stopped in front of a Degas oil, still feeling like an observer who wanted to dance with the ballerinas, but couldn't find the courage to join them.

Nope. That was the old attitude, the choking lack of self-esteem she'd been a servant to for most of her life.

If she was so empowered by moving out and taking control, why couldn't she march back up to Rick Shane and straighten things out with *him*?

Daisy, he'd said at the pier. *If you ever need me, day or night, you know where I am.*

Her heartbeat popped in her chest, shortening her breath.

Briefly, she wondered if she was trading one addiction for another, replacing food with the human touch, filling her hollow center with whatever worked.

Absolutely not. Food had never made her feel wanted. Not like Rick had. And when he'd fixed his dark gaze on her in St. Louis, on the edge of unburdening himself of something so painful he couldn't even stand to make love to her…

Okay, on some level, maybe she did need to be with him in order to fulfill herself. But, right now, analyzing her desire wasn't doing any good.

She wouldn't be able to sleep unless she was near him tonight. Is that what he'd meant by saying that he'd be there for her? She hoped so.

Minutes later, after making sure Tarkin and Coral were abed, she was on her way to Rick's place. Everybody in Kane's Crossing knew where everyone else lived, so she had no problem finding her way. She just couldn't get there fast enough.

As she parked and got out of her car, the endless black sky cloaked her, made her almost invisible among the rustling leaves and the hoot of an owl. Chilly air carried the scent of pine and wood smoke, but Daisy couldn't see anything coming from the chimney, couldn't see movement beyond his window panes in the darkness of his home.

Was he even here? God, she'd feel like a fool if she had to creep back into Peter's home, rejected and lonely.

Rick kept his door unlocked. Daisy remembered that little nugget from the day she'd run from her wedding and he'd taken her here.

Should she go inside? His Jeep was here, nestled under a shingled overhang on the side of the cabin.

Daisy, she told herself. You are the new improved version of *you*. Just do it.

She took care to make barely any noise as she thudded up the wooden stairs, took care to negotiate the moaning hinges as she opened the door.

Embers glowed in his fireplace, watching her like the unblinking eye of a preternatural guard dog. The smell of beer twined around the discarded brown bottles tipping over the sofa and end table.

As she eased open the door a bit farther, a slit of moonlight spread over the clothing slumped on the floor, over a sheeted lump in the corner bed.

Daisy's pulse skittered, flailing with ungraceful urgency down her veins. He *was* home, sleeping.

While her brain told her scram back to safety, her body kicked her yearning into overdrive.

After pushing the door closed, she doffed her flats, all the better to sneak with.

And sneak she did, right next to his bed.

She stood over him, unwilling to disturb the peace of his slumber. He had his head turned toward the wall, his ruffled sable hair winged against the pillow, his lips slightly parted. Shaded whiskers surrounded his mouth, stumps of a burned forest. With one arm tossed over his head and the other wrapped around an extra pillow, Rick Shane seemed almost vulnerable, in need of care.

Daisy's gaze moved lower, past his sparsely furred chest, coasting to the stream of hair that bisected his belly and disappeared beneath the crease of a white sheet. Not long ago, she'd traced that downy trail, feeling his skin quiver under her fingertips.

God help her, she wanted to touch him again.

She extended her hand, reaching for him, wanting to feel his heat under her palm.

When she leaned against the bed to balance herself, the mattress shifted a fraction. But it was enough to jar him into wakefulness.

His actions blurred together, all happening at seemingly the same instant. One hand whipped out, banding around her wrist with bruising intensity. He bolted forward into a sitting position, the sheet draping over his hips. He pulled her toward him, bringing her eye to eye with him, his glare shooting off shards of black ice. His other hand darted around her throat. Fear shot through her.

Choking. Peter. Running.

His thumb pressed against her windpipe, robbing her of breath.

"Rick?" she choked.

He'd bared his teeth, all but snarling at her. For a second, Daisy thought he was truly going to strangle her, but then, something snapped in his gaze. He pushed back from her, releasing his hold.

"Goddammit, Daisy."

She sat on the bed, rubbing the rawness of her throat, knowing she'd been stupid to creep up on him like that.

What haunted his sleep, forcing him to fight his way out of it?

"Jeez." He fumbled a hand toward her, but Daisy flinched from his touch.

She whispered, the effort making her tender throat feel bruised. "I'm so sorry. I didn't mean to scare you like that."

"What the hell are you doing here?"

He was so hard and beautiful at the same time, his body carved with brawny ridges and sinew, the sheet barely hiding any of it. Daisy could see the beginning of his arousal beneath the cotton, and she looked away.

What had she been doing here? She'd wanted to lie near him, to feel his heartbeat against her cheek, to nestle into the comfort of his strong arms. But how could she put those feelings into words?

"I just wanted to be with you," she said.

He ran his hands over his face, hiding behind the shield of his fingers. His voice muffled its way out from the barrier. "I suppose I was having a nightmare."

No kidding. Daisy experimentally touched her throat, wincing a little at a phantom pressure that still burned her skin. "If I were to guess, I'd say that your head is full of bad dreams."

Leaning back against his pillows, Rick let his hands fall away from his face. Then, slowly, he laid his fingertips against her neck. "I didn't mean to hurt you, Daisy. I'd never consciously do that."

"I know."

He dropped his hands to his sheeted thighs, peered out the bedside window, skeletal trees casting spindly fingers of shadow over his eyes. Her heart ached for him, literally. It was scratching its way out of her chest, clawing for recognition.

He said, "From the way you acted yesterday, at the arcade, I didn't think you wanted anything to do with me."

"You're wrong."

"You ran away again."

She shifted on the bed, agonizingly aware that he wasn't wearing anything beneath the sheets, explosively mindful that he was only inches from her skin. "I'm so confused that I don't know what to do." She laughed. "But at least I'm leaving Peter's home."

"About time." He clenched his hands, his gaze moving from the window to his fists, probably remembering how he'd just about choked the life out of her, how Peter had threatened to do the same.

"You were the one who set things up with Lacey, right? You talked her into letting me stay at her place."

He didn't say anything, just kept watching his hands.

He didn't have to answer for her to know that it was true.

"Rick…?"

He drew in a great, shuddering breath. "What do you want from me?"

"I…" Be careful, she thought. How far do you intend to go?

She swallowed. "I want to know why you couldn't

make love to me the other night. I know it's so silly. But this is something I just can't shake. I need this.''

Needed to know for sure that she didn't turn him off with her full-figured body. Needed to know that she could help him as much as he'd helped her.

After all, when you loved someone, you did everything you could to keep them happy.

Right?

Rick cursed, looking away from her to the window again. Daisy tried not to allow his reticence to affect her.

Slowly, as if approaching a wounded animal, she placed her palm on his shin, feeling the shape of muscle curve beneath her extended fingers and the smooth sheet. She rubbed there soothingly, hearing his breathing pick up its pace.

Her movements spoke louder than her voice ever could.

I'm listening.

''You can't begin to understand how ugly it is inside of me,'' he said, his voice low enough to barely edge out the sound of a shutter banging against a shed outside.

''Why?'' She scratched over his calf, behind his knee, nailing him gently.

He stirred, and she couldn't help gauging the bulge between his legs. Her lower belly flared in response.

He answered with a sharp laugh. ''Because everything about you is perfect, even if you don't think so.''

She'd denied this before. Doing it again would take the conversation in a direction that exhausted her.

Instead, she stroked higher, right above the knee.

He put his hand over hers. "You're gonna think I'm crazy for saying this, but I've got this misguided notion that I've got to earn you."

She smiled and shook her head. "What are you talking about?"

He hesitated. "Let's just say that I haven't done a very good job of handling relationships in the past. Will that be enough for you?"

She should've said yes, but her heart wouldn't settle for that. "No. I want to know why you beat yourself down every once in a while. I want to know why there's a pit of darkness in the middle of your eyes."

"Darkness." His tone mocked the word. "You make me sound complicated."

She ignored his attempt at misdirecting the conversation. "What did you do after high school, Rick? No one around here seems to know."

From the jagged cut of the lines around his mouth, she'd hit her target.

"Do we have to talk about this?" He traced a thumb over the sensitive valley between her thumb and forefinger, sending shivers over the hairs of her skin.

"I wish we would. Some people say you ran off to join the marines."

His answer slashed right out. "Army."

"There we go." She grinned, skimming her hand

a few inches higher, traveling the clean lines of his inner thigh.

He groaned, reclining his head against the wall and shutting his eyelids. "I fought in the Gulf War. Not much more to tell than that."

Daisy couldn't imagine life in a war zone. Couldn't imagine Rick there, either.

She ran her gaze over his body. "Why don't you have any scars? Don't soldiers get tattoos?"

"Not everyone. And scars aren't just physical." He cut himself off, as if he'd said too much. "I was lucky. Walked out of there unscathed, pretty much." He paused. "Then, after my tour, I headed down to Hawaii and flew tourists around Kauai for a few bucks."

He shifted his knee, and she realized that she'd stopped paying attention to his leg. She started rubbing again. "Hawaii? Why'd you come back to Kane's Crossing?"

"My dad." Rick pressed his lips together, then said, "He died, and I thought being with the family, trying to mend some hurts, would be the right thing to do."

"Did you? Mend hurts, I mean."

"It was too late with the old man. I'm starting to succeed with Matth...Matt, but it's been a long time in coming."

Daisy wondered what had happened in the Gulf. He'd skipped over that part pretty quickly. But something told her not to ask.

She smiled, thinking now was a good time to

lighten the mood. "Did you break many hearts on your journey around the world?"

"What makes you think my heart hasn't sustained any damage?"

An opening. She gathered her courage. "What was her name?"

He must've known what she was getting at. "Specialist Clarice Hopkins. But forget that. I've tried to erase every military gesture, habit, piece of clothing from my life. Okay, Daisy? Can we not talk about this?"

Heck, she'd gotten enough for tonight, she supposed.

When she glanced back at him, his gaze resembled an open wound—raw, assailable to more pain.

She crawled up the bed while he slid downward, grooving back into the indentation he'd carved from many previous slumbers. Daisy noticed that there wasn't a matching one on her side of the bed. The thought both saddened and gladdened her.

He plucked at her long sweater while she tugged down her skirt.

"You're wrong. You're not ugly," she said. "Not anywhere. Outside, inside, you're just fine with me."

Rick didn't say a word.

Daisy guided her palm over his stomach, feeling the furrows of muscle tense under her skin. Then she continued upward, over his rib cage, over the hair under his arm.

He twitched, and she kissed the line of his jaw, making him groan.

They lay there, enjoying the touch of each other.

But then, he had to explore, had to smooth over the flab of her stomach. She pulled away ever so slightly.

"What?" he asked.

"Nothing."

He paused. "Are you afraid that I'm thinking you've got a few extra pounds?"

Shame suffused her face and body with heat. She almost hopped off the bed then, but he grabbed her, holding her tightly against him.

"Don't do that, Daisy. Don't let anybody make you feel any less than you are."

"Well, there's a lot to me, you know."

She could feel him shaking his head.

"I was…" She cleared her throat. "I am bulimic. Hating myself comes with the territory."

For a minute, she thought he was going to ask her what bulimia was. But he didn't, thank goodness. She didn't think she had it in her to go into the awful details.

He said, "I dated a woman who did that. She was actually hospitalized for it."

"I never got that far."

"How could you do that to yourself?" Rick asked, pulling her body closer to his. His pulse was still pounding from earlier in the night, when she'd stolen into his house, uninvited.

He could've killed himself for bringing Daisy into his nightmare, reaching for her throat, acting out his aggression for something that had happened years ago.

Iraqi soldiers, armed to the teeth, crushing down on him and the men who fought by his side, overwhelming them with fire and blood...

He cleared his brain, realizing that Daisy had as much to hide as he did.

Bulimia was a secretive, addictive disorder. His ex-girlfriend, a casual fling really, had explained this when he'd heard her throwing up in his bathroom in Hawaii. He also knew that bulimia could really jar your body out of whack.

In a matter-of-fact tone, Daisy said, "I'm okay now, although every once in a while, I start giving into the stress, wanting to be perfect. That's when I feel like doing it."

"It's hard to understand."

"Tell me about it. It was never the food that was important. It was the loss of emotion when I'd sit in front of the TV, eating and eating. Then I'd realize how many calories I'd consumed...." She wrapped an arm around his middle. "That was a long time ago."

He squeezed her against his chest, protecting her from memories.

She said, "That's how I maintained my weight throughout most of my teenage years. A lot of girls on the circuit did it. Then came the Miss America debacle and it got worse. I did it during my spokes-modeling jobs, too. I'd tell myself that I could stop at any time. Any time."

She paused, sighing. "Then, after years of abusing myself, I realized that I couldn't stop after all."

He tried to imagine how she'd messed herself up inside, just as he had.

They were both hurting in places no one else saw.

"How did you get over it?" he asked, wondering if he could ever find the strength she had.

"I began seeing a therapist on my own. It didn't help that I could barely pay for the doctor. We were in a tight spot with our budget, and so much of our money had to go toward working off Peter's loan. But then I stopped. I gained weight, lost the spokes-modeling job and made the unfortunate decision to marry the wrong man. But I overcame that."

Emotion welled in his throat, choking back his words. Instead, he pressed his lips to her forehead.

He only wished he could spell out, *I'm so proud of you* with his kisses.

Maybe she understood, though. Her answering kiss warmed him to the core, making his body heat rise until alarm bells shook the walls of his brain.

He could hardly believe that he was naked in bed, with a fully dressed Daisy Cox by his side. Why wasn't his libido laughing at him by now?

Probably because he'd been convinced enough— by Daisy's persuasive hands—to tell her a few details about *his* life. The further her fingers had flitted up his thigh, the more he'd talked.

She'd have been a brilliant torture master in the days of yore, huh?

He glanced over at Daisy, desire spiking through

him when he saw one of her curls dancing over the pillow. He wanted to wind his finger up in it, wanted to brush his mouth against her neck, smelling the breeze of her meadow shampoo.

Instead, he listened as her breathing evened out, filling his cabin with sound and life.

As he shut his eyes and tugged at the sheet to cover Daisy, he thought that maybe she belonged right here.

In his home.

Chapter Twelve

Hours must have passed since Daisy snuggled into bed with Rick, because the sky was beginning to show the first signs of stretching awake. Hints of orange and purple yawned across the still-dark horizon, making Rick think that this might be a great Cessna day.

Daisy adjusted her position beside him, her skirt sneaking up to the middle of her soft thighs, her hands loosely balled against the chest of her sweater.

She'd kicked off the sheets again. Daggonit, if there was one thing that chapped Rick's hide, it was a cover kicker.

He waited until she scrunched up her nose and peeked at him. "Where am I?"

"My own personal hell, where someone creeped in last night and stole all my covers."

Daisy gave a cute laugh, making Rick grin, too.

"It's a bad habit," she said.

"It happened at least ten times. I was about to throw you out of bed."

"Not for eatin' crackers." She propped herself on her forearm, seeming surprised when she saw that she still had on her clothing.

When she glanced at him in wonder, he merely tossed up his hands. "Maybe I'm a nice guy after all."

"I'm still sleepy. Give me a second to come up with some clever arguments for that one."

Her golden hair tufted around her face. Rick flicked a spiraled lock with his finger. "You've got bed head."

Daisy smoothed back some wayward strands. "Well, Rick Shane. You know the worst about me now. I wake up looking like someone ran me over with an eighteen wheeler."

He chuckled. "Sounds like an ideal pageant event. Bathing suit, talent, evening gown and rolling-out-of-bed competition."

"Don't make fun of it. The pageants do a lot of charity work and give out scholarships." She used an index finger to further her point, shaking it in the air. "The public doesn't realize that contestants in the Miss America pageant even write social-issue essays, you know. The women have to adopt a platform, almost like a politician. You actually have to use your brain."

She capped off that burst of energy with a delicate yawn.

Rick pressed a hand over his heart in mock sympathy. "Forgive my incorrigibility, Miss Daisy."

She lay back on the bed, shutting her eyes. "I could've really used one of those scholarships."

He nodded, not knowing what to say. Her life would've changed if she'd gone to college. She most likely wouldn't have been anywhere near his bed right now.

Pushing aside his selfish reasoning, Rick leaned over, tracing a fingertip over her cheekbone. Her skin was what you'd imagine a cloud was like when you were a kid, when you sat on the ground watching the wispy puffs dance past you. Soft, warm, heavenly.

She kept her eyes shut. "I've got to go, Rick."

He glanced at an old school-style clock poised on a wall by his bed. With the help of the faint outside light, he could barely read the hands.

"It's early. I suppose Tarkin's pacing the floor, waiting for you."

"Maybe. Dracula doesn't sleep until dawn."

Trouble was, Rick had a tough time slumbering, too. But last night, after Daisy had settled into his bed, finding peace with her warm, fragrant body snuggled next to his had been easy.

Too easy.

He lunged beneath the sheets again, and Daisy scooted over, nestling a leg between both of his sheet-covered ones, wrapping an arm around his waist.

His heartbeat kicked into high gear, pumping blood to his lower regions.

She had to know that she was turning him on. Even her slightest move was enough to send tiny explosions through his body.

"Thought you had to go," he said.

"I really do." She tilted her chin up, watching him, her breath heating his neck.

He peered down at Daisy, her eyes wide and dark, her lips a feather's tip away from his.

Rick wasn't sure who moved first, but they were kissing before he could blink his eyes shut. During the lazy slide of both their mouths crushing together, he rolled Daisy on top of him, hands buried in the wealth of her soft hair.

As they tasted each other, sucking and nibbling, Daisy gently wiggled her hips over his stiffness, making him want to impale her right then and there. Through the thin sheet, he could feel the moist heat between her legs, could feel that she was ready for him, even this early in the game.

The central heating kicked on from a vent located over his bed. The air moaned around them, heightening the effect of Daisy's kisses. As she rocked against him, winding her hands in his hair, she darted her tongue into his mouth, teasing him in time to the sway of her hips.

Rick smoothed his hands under her sweater, over her bare back, tracing the bumps of her spine until he got to her bra clasp. With a deftness culled from lots of unsnapped lingerie, he loosened the material, skimming his fingertips around her waist until he reached her stomach.

She moaned as he sucked on her tongue, ending the kiss, taking it new places, sliding his mouth down the column of her throat, nosing aside a few damp curls until he found the pulse of her vein. Then up, to her ear, toying with the shell of it, exploring the ridges, breathing into it with ever-increasing urgency.

As she leaned into his mouth, Daisy shivered, then roamed her hand over his chest, using her thumb to circle his aching nipple.

He murmured, "Don't you have to go?"

She laughed, stretching up until she was straddling him. "I'll suffer the consequences."

While Rick grinned and languidly caressed her thighs, gliding under her skirt to spread her legs even farther, Daisy whisked off her sweater, tossing it to the floor. The bra dangled from her arms, and she made quick work of that, too.

She hesitated, and Rick could feel the taut indecision of her body.

To help her along, he insinuated his thumbs along her inner thighs, to the skin hidden by her conservative skirt. He rubbed along her curves, drawn to the heat between her legs.

She had no idea about how she worked him into a frenzy, did she? Right now, she was probably wondering if he'd stop making love to her again, wondering if she was attractive enough to keep him going this time.

Hell, tonight he wouldn't stop. Not for anything.

As he pressed a thumb against the middle of her underwear, swirling against her telltale wetness, Daisy arched her neck, her lips parting as she gasped.

Outside, faint light angled awake, slanting through the window with a murky hue, allowing Rick to appreciate Daisy's body all the more.

With grainy purity, the morning spectrum filtered over her breasts, blasting a furnace of hunger through Rick's body. With one hand still stroking the spot between her legs, he used his other to cup a swollen mound.

It spilled out of his palm with its fullness and, as her nipples peaked, Daisy grasped his wrist, scratching down his arm as if to encourage him.

"More," she said, cupping his other hand so that he was palming the center of her.

Urged by a lightning flash of lust, Rick rose from his position, gently pushing Daisy backward until she lay flush against the mattress, cradled by his arms. He worked her skirt off while fastening his mouth to a hardened nipple, laving his tongue over it, sipping as if taking all her brightness into him.

He could feel air from the vent comb over his bare backside, could smell the lavender-laced soap Daisy used. Everything bloomed inside with more vivid colors, sharpening his senses.

As he slid his tongue around her breasts, grazing his teeth over the underside and causing her to grab his hair and clamp her legs around his own, Rick felt something fist within his belly. A tightness, an inferno licking at the edges of his common sense.

No, dammit. He was with Daisy now. Nothing was going to stop him from making love with her this time.

Daisy was doing that wiggle again, the one that made him just want to drive into her and spend himself.

She slicked down his sweat-coated body, the silk of her underwear grazing his length, pushing him to his last nerve.

"I want to feel you against me," she said, shifting, her ample breasts flattening as she pressed against him.

His own nipples were sensitized, sending zings of desire through every pore of his skin. "Daisy..."

He buried his face in her hair, breathing in her summer sweetness, cutting off ill-advised words whipped up by their contact. His sharpened emotions were pushing him to do stupid things. Things that had a price.

She ran her palms up his back, grinding against him, breathless. "I've got protection in the pocket of my skirt," she whispered.

If Rick weren't so busy trying to hold back his urges, he might've been impressed. With a low moan, he backed away from Daisy, quickly searching the skirt for the promised condoms. He, himself, had a box of them in his bathroom, but he'd explode before he got there.

Two foil packages. "You had this *all* planned out," he said, grinning.

"I'm trying to finish what I start."

She propped herself up on her elbows, reminding Rick of the hotel room, of her on the table in the same position. The only difference was, this time, she wasn't watching him with that hurtful blue gaze.

He grasped one packet in his hand, easing back onto the bed, tearing it open.

Before going any further, he glanced at Daisy, running his gaze over her as if she could feel the caress of his appreciation.

Hair wildly askew, breasts hardened from his touch, soft belly, damnable underwear...

She lay back, covering her chest and stomach with her arms. "Don't look at me that way."

"What way?"

"I..." She glanced away, still keeping herself covered.

He set down the condom, laying his body over hers again. "When are you going to understand that I want you the way you are?"

"It's just hard to believe."

Dammit. His heart was jackhammering its way down his body, taking the scenic route and no doubt intending to settle in his groin, throbbing there like a time bomb. He didn't know if he had the strength to hold back.

Rick cupped Daisy's chin, turning her gaze back to him. "Your body is beautiful."

He took both her hands, guiding them away from her skin until her arms rested on the bed. She almost looked like she wanted to embrace something.

Then he coasted a palm down the length of her body. "You couldn't be more perfect for me."

Too late, he wished he'd left off the "for me" part. It seemed just on the precipice of admitting to something he wasn't willing to give.

As his touch skimmed down to her underwear, he tenderly slipped his thumbs under the elastic on both sides, coaxing the material downward, far enough so that he could fling the silky briefs away.

They locked gazes as Rick parted her legs, trailing his fingers over the inside of her thighs, touching the center of her, working into her slick folds, knowing she was ready for him.

She reached for the protection. "Let me put it on."

And she did, leading it over every inch by throbbing inch. Then he settled against her body, prodding her.

With one of those wiggles, Daisy took him inside her warmth, hesitating, tightening around him as they started to move together.

They danced under a prom-night moon, with all the snapshot heat of his teenage fantasies. As their sweat mingled, making their skin skid against each other, they graduated to a lazy jazz beat, the tempo quickening with every thrust.

In a dizzy vortex of curled smoke and soulful sax notes, Rick watched Daisy's face as she flushed beneath the waning predawn light, watched as she lost herself in the ecstasy they were both sharing, creating.

Damn, he couldn't hold back any longer, couldn't hold off the insistent need for release.

As he shut his eyes, he flew, touching the sky with a fingertip, tracing the clouds until he started falling, the ground zooming toward him with dangerous speed.

As he hit, the world imploded, bursting open as Rick spent himself.

He collected his feelings, having shattered them all over the place during the encounter. While Daisy shifted beneath him, Rick tightened his lips, refusing to spill out any promises.

Holding back the confusion he felt about making love with Daisy.

He pleasured her with his fingers, his mouth, until she crashed to earth, too, panting and grasping at him, holding him to her as her heartbeat fluttered against his own skin.

He kissed her, pressing her close as their breathing evened out together.

Bringing each other down to a place where he had no business thinking that he'd made the right choice tonight.

They'd done it.

Daisy tried to control the trembling that had started in her stomach and spread to every other part of her body. She almost felt cold, but warm at the same time, her limbs aching and jarred, but pleasantly sensitive.

Rick still held her, his strong arms pressing her against his chest, his lips against her forehead.

What was there to say? She hadn't had a lot of experience in after-glow training, not since she'd made a fool of herself during her experimental teen-age phase.

Making love with another man hadn't been high on her list of things to accomplish. And, besides, she hadn't the courage to shed her clothing in front of just any candidate.

Yeah. Rick was the one she'd been waiting for. Gently aggressive. Intensely tender.

She only wished he returned her feelings, because now, she knew she was in love. She'd known it since St. Louis, but tonight had been the capper.

The sky had lightened even more, reminding Daisy that she needed to get to "the house"—she refused to call it "home" anymore—ASAP.

She stirred, loosening Rick's hold on her. "Really. This time I need to leave."

"Right."

He grinned at her as she rose from the bed and, if she peered hard enough, she could detect a slight downturn of his mouth. A crooked sign of—what was it? Regret?

Daisy, don't even think that way.

As she gathered her clothes, she tried so hard to feel natural about being undressed in front of him. But she couldn't help rushing into her undies, her bra, the skirt and sweater.

Heck, he was still naked as a jaybird. And, from the sight of it, he could give a flying fig.

No, she thought, don't look at him. You'll just be tempted to want more than he's offering right now.

But, deep in her heart, she knew that there was a

chance to break through to him, to sweep off his dark shroud and get to the spark of his soul. To make him forget about whatever haunted him.

There. Dressed. Done. What now? See you later? Thanks for the good time, Mac?

"I've, uh, I've got to get going," she said, finding her shoes and stepping back into them.

Oh, that was clever. She'd only repeated her need to leave about twenty-two times.

She huffed out a sigh. "Would you get some clothes on?"

He shrugged while still lying there. "I'm going back to bed."

You can join me, too, his tone intimated.

"All right." Daisy flipped up a hand in a lame gesture of farewell, then cracked open the door.

His voice cut over the crisp morning air. "You're not going to marry Tarkin?"

After all that and he still had to ask? "What do you think?"

"Just making sure."

She couldn't believe he still had so little faith in her. The decision to call off her marriage was looking smarter every moment, and he didn't see that.

"I'm sorry my choice wasn't more obvious," she said. Then, with a slam, she shut the door on him.

As she speed-walked back to her car, Daisy berated herself. This had been a joke to Rick. Maybe he'd even been testing her resolve in that arrogant way of his.

God, had she made another mistake? This time with *him?*

His door banged against the wall while she jerked open her car. Rick stood there, his lower body wrapped in the sheet. While they stared at each other, he walked toward her.

He wasn't joking anymore. She could tell by the stern set of his jaw, by the liquid dark of his eyes.

When he stopped in front of her, Daisy's gaze traveled to his chest. The early light cast a surreal, gray hue over his skin. She could see that his nipples were tightened by the chilly morning, and she couldn't help remembering the feel of them against her own breasts.

He said, "I wasn't poking fun at you. I know you're gonna leave that house and use all your strength to start a new life, Daisy."

"Yeah, I will." And that life had started last night for her.

He leaned in, planting a hand in her hair, fixing his mouth to hers in a slow, aching kiss. The slick heat of it was almost enough to get her back into the cabin, back into his bed.

He smelled of afterglow musk and traces of soap, dragging her down to his will once again.

All too soon, he ended the caress, pressing his forehead to Daisy's, playing with the ringlets at the nape of her neck.

They didn't say anything for a full minute, instead matching each other breath for breath.

Then, without a word, she got into her car, started

the engine and did a U-turn in order to drive the lane that led away from his secluded cabin.

As she left, she could see him in the rearview mirror, standing there, wrapped in his sheet, watching as she drove to the place she didn't dare call ''home.''

When Daisy arrived back at Peter's house, she used every secret-agent skill she could muster: coasting the car into its garaged parking space, quietly sneaking through the back door so no one would hear her.

Evidently, it was still too early for Peter and Coral to be up and about. With any luck, she wouldn't have been missed. After all, it's not like anyone did bed checks on her. And Peter, rumored gentleman that he was, had adamantly insisted that they wait until their wedding night to sleep together.

Ugh. The thought of it gave Daisy the hives.

All in all, chances were good that her night-time trip to Rick's wouldn't be noted.

While shedding her clothes, Daisy had to swerve around her packed boxes, which were waiting to be moved to Lacey's house. She hopped into her bed, unable to get to sleep. So she daydreamed, staring at the ceiling, imagining what Rick had done to her body, replaying the entire event.

When seven o'clock, her normal waking time, rolled around, she jumped out of bed to shower, then dressed and went downstairs for breakfast.

Another soft-boiled egg awaited her, along with Coral and Peter, who were engrossed in their own omelets and the morning paper.

They all muttered a "good morning" to each other as Daisy took her seat at the end of the stretching, linen-lined table. Only Coral peeked up from her paper, a pair of black-framed reading glasses perched on her nose, a frown marring her face.

Ewww. Daisy didn't like that expression. She'd seen it a couple times before. The most vivid memories came to mind: once, when Becky had chopped off Daisy's bangs, and again, when Daisy had gone out with the boy who'd helped ruin her pageant career.

With studied ease, Daisy smiled at Coral, and her sister went back to reading the paper.

"Daisy." Peter stamped out her name, demanding her attention as he lowered his own *Kane's Crossing Gazette.*

She snapped to attention, a bad omen gnawing at the lining of her stomach. "Yes?"

He took the time to crease the paper with exceptional care. Daisy noticed that his business suit matched the crisp folds of it.

Coral merely dumped her own *Gazette* on the floor, where it probably belonged in the first place.

Darn gossip rag. She'd read those wedding excuse articles. They'd said Daisy had suffered from a "temporary attack of the nerves," when she'd run away from the altar.

Fair reporting, indeed.

Peter patted his mouth with his napkin, and Daisy awaited her sentence. Just *let* him chastise her for being out all night.

"Daisy, I've been called out on one of those sudden business trips. The wedding planner, whom you left sitting here Saturday, will be returning tomorrow. I expect you to be here and not leave Coral with the duties of preparation."

He *expected* it. How could she have listened to him talk to her like this in the past? Had she really been that spineless?

Coral shot her a quelling glare, but there was something odd about it. Something Daisy couldn't quite put her finger on.

She wasn't exactly scolding her but...

Daisy ignored the warning. "What is this trip about?" Might as well be sweet now because, when he got back, she wouldn't be living here.

Peter seemed miffed that she'd even presume to ask his business. She hadn't ever done so before.

"It's none of your concern, Daisy. You just concentrate on repairing your reputation in this town."

He rose from his seat. "Oh, one more thing. I've left a menu for you. It's a diet prescribed by your doctor."

Stick to it.

The nerve of him. Didn't he know that she was perfect for the man who'd made love to her last night?

Every brain cell screamed for her to tell Peter that she was moving out, that she wouldn't in a million years marry him.

But Coral caught Daisy's eye. Warning her.

She kept her tongue, at least on that subject.

Daisy picked up her spoon and smashed it into the

egg. Little did Peter know that she imagined it was actually *his* head she was decimating.

She smiled up at him, all sweetness and light. "Have a wonderful trip."

As he left the room, she realized that he hadn't said anything about her being gone last night. Daisy sank into her seat, hardly believing her luck.

Coral watched her, and Daisy had the feeling she was in for a speech.

"He was in a snit this morning," she said. "I didn't want you to make any waves, Dizzy."

Daisy waited for Coral to lower the boom, to say, "I know what you did last night."

But it wasn't forthcoming.

Coral sniffed, doffing her glasses and cleaning them with a napkin. "We can't afford to anger Peter. Especially now."

The last words sounded ominous, but Daisy didn't ask for more information. She knew what she was up against with her ex-fiancé.

As Daisy ate her grotesque egg, she did her best to hide a secret that Coral couldn't even fathom.

She was in love. And it wasn't with Peter.

Chapter Thirteen

The following weekend, during the annual town anniversary at Kane Spencer Hall, the garbage hit the fan.

At least, that's what Rick thought when he saw the tacky decorations littering the inside of the building.

Long red-white-and-blue streamers hung from the oak molding around the ceiling, the paper's listless fingers scratching the heads of partygoers as they mingled on the polished wooden floor. Cardboard cut-outs, supposedly resembling the town founder, wobbled on the stage, located near the Ladies Auxiliary refreshment table, by the door. White plastic fold-out chairs lined the area, reminding Rick of skeletal hangers just waiting for a fancy suit to flop over them.

What was he doing in a place like this?

Once more, he surveyed the floor, but he didn't find the only person he wanted to see.

Daisy.

A female voice brought him back to reality. "She'll be here soon," said his stepsister, Lacey.

She'd gotten gussied up in a sooty ankle-length Audrey Hepburn dress, complete with the black gloves and a costume-jewelry tiara nestled in her upswept hair.

He grinned at his sibling. "You watch *Breakfast at Tiffany's* again?"

"Don't avoid the subject." She propped a long cigarette holder that she wasn't actually smoking against her lower lip. "Daisy needed to freshen up before we attended this poor excuse for a soiree. You didn't go to the wagon races this afternoon like we did."

Hell, Rick hadn't ever attended any of the Kane Spencer festivities. No apple-pie baking contests, no bluegrass music picnics, no street fairs for him. Coming to this end-of-the-celebration gathering was enough. Besides, last night, Daisy had said she'd be here.

And his body demanded that he see her again. And again. And…

Rick stopped himself, shrugging. "I'm not a wagon-racing kind of guy."

"I wonder if you really know what kind of guy you are," said Lacey.

He realized one thing for sure. He wasn't the settling type. Every minute, every hour he'd spent with Daisy this week, when she'd come to his cabin at night and they'd make love until morning, told him so.

When he held her, his body aching from their spent passion, she still watched him with questions in her eyes. Rick knew she wanted him to tell her about his past, his hurts, just as she'd done about her own mortifying secret—the bulimia.

But she didn't understand that his anguish was something better left unsaid, untouched. Better left buried in the corner of his mind, where it breathed during the dark of night, where it waited for him to ruin it with Daisy so Rick could return to the nightmares.

A chill scraped down his spine, and he must have shuddered.

Lacey tugged on his bomber jacket. "You okay?"

"Yeah."

"Oh." She peeked across the room. "Because I thought you just saw Daisy's sister walk in."

Rick followed Lacey's gaze, resting his own on the woman who helped herself to the contents of the snack table. A faded version of Daisy, this sister had been ripped off by the gene pool when it came to the beauty her younger sibling had been born with.

Lacey said, "Coral's none too happy about Daisy moving to my place. Of course, I invited her to live with us, too, but she's a stubborn one. Won't hear of it."

"She still wants Daisy to marry Tarkin. Doesn't she?"

"That's what Daisy says." Lacey tapped him with

her cigarette. "Don't you talk about this sort of thing with her?"

Guilt burned over him. When he was with Daisy, he did his best to steer the action away from conversation. He didn't trust what might come out of his mouth.

All he knew for sure was that she wasn't living under Tarkin's thumb anymore. That she was safe, for the time being.

"Hey!" Lacey pulled on his arm, toward the doors. "There're the girls, dragging along the smitten hubbies."

Indeed, Meg and Nick Cassidy, Ashlyn and Sheriff Sam Reno, and Rachel and Matt had arrived, sans children. Rick supposed that the Widow Antle, who worked in Meg's bakery, was taking care of the brood.

Matt, his cowboy hat draped low over his brow, spotted his brother, nodding. His gesture seemed full of meaning, and Rick thought back to the other day, when they'd cleared away some of the bad memories between them.

He jerked his chin at Matt, feeling for the first time in years that it wasn't a forced gesture.

A group of feisty teenage kids pranced between them, blocking Rick's view. Just as one football-jacketed lunkhead cuffed another on the side of the head, someone shouted, "There's Sheriff Reno!" and the group dispersed.

In the aftermath, a boy thunked to the ground, laughing up a storm. One of his friends returned, dragging him to his feet. If Rick didn't know any better, he'd say that the kid was drunk.

"Nice," said Lacey. "I wonder who's got the flask."

"Don't look at me," said Rick, hands in the air.

"I wasn't— Oh!" Lacey hid behind him. "Pretend I'm not here."

Good God. Where was Daisy? Now he knew why he didn't come to these damned things. Too much drama.

"What's wrong?" he asked.

Lacey whispered, "See those people who just walked in?"

Yup. A barrel-chested man with broad, Teutonic features strolled through the entrance as if he owned the place, fingers grasping his tailored lapels, pale blond hair sparkling under the lights like platinum plating. His equally royal companions circled around him, providing a moving shield as he made his way into the party.

It had to be Johann Spencer, the European relative who'd purchased the remaining Spencer property once Horatio and Edwina had betrayed their daughter, Ashlyn. They'd left the country due to the consequences of their criminal activities concerning the toy factory, and Johann hadn't wasted any time taking up where the Kane's Crossing Spencers had left off.

Lacey was still hiding. "Johann's out to wring my neck."

"What'd you do now?" Though he'd spoken with a light tone, Rick could feel himself gearing up to protect Lacey, just as he'd done throughout their childhood, when people had ridden her for being "odd."

"I bought some of their old land. You know, the abandoned warehouse by the general store? Johann wants every speck of Spencer property back, but I told him no. I'm not selling out to him."

"Land? Lacey, what're you going to do with more land? You've already got a business to run, a nice big house to live in."

"You're not going to believe it when I tell you." Lacey came around in front of him, a huge smile on her lips.

"Why am I not going to like this?" asked Rick.

She twirled her cigarette holder. "I'm commissioning an architect to build a glass castle on the property."

He waited for further explanation, and she smiled innocently at him.

"Don't worry. It's nothing that'll put me back in Hazy Lawn Clinic. I just want to build a castle for the kids at the Reno Center, and use the admission fees to raise money for scholarships."

Rick thought there might be more to it than that. "Don't tell me you're hell bent on making yourself look like an upstanding citizen or something."

Gaze softening, she opened her mouth to speak, then closed it, widening her eyes. "Here comes Johann. I'll explain more later." Pecking him on the cheek, she said, "Bye."

As she left, Rick locked his sights on Johann, stepping into his line of vision so he could block Lacey's retreat.

Across the room, Johann scanned him with a cool glance, then directed his attention back to his company. Dismissed.

Good riddance.

Rick checked the clock at the rear of the room, wondering if Daisy would show up at his cabin tonight if he left this party. She'd asked him to be here, and he wondered if she wanted to use him to show Kane's Crossing that she didn't belong to Tarkin anymore.

Not that Rick minded being used. He couldn't give her any more than what he was giving her now—secret meetings, twisted sheets, silent afterglows.

Bringing himself to fall in love with her was out of the question. Long ago he'd had his chance at love, and he'd come out as something less than human.

Something that didn't even deserve what he and Daisy had now.

Tap, tap, tap. The mayor had stepped on stage, beating the microphone with sausage-thick fingers.

From underneath the fall of his gray walrus mustache, the man rolled back on his heels and hooked his fingers in his vest, waiting for the audience's attention.

When he had it, he started with a ''Good evening, folks!''

The Ladies' Auxiliary clapped fervently at the refreshment table while the high-school kids booed. One or two of them had even climbed to the rafters, swinging their legs, making monkey noises. Another two kids stumbled out the door, arm in arm.

As the mayor announced the night's schedule—first the award ribbons for the week's contests, then a concert from the Retired Toy Factory Swinger Band— Rick kept watching the doorway, almost as if he could feel Daisy walking in before she actually did.

Seconds later, she was there, golden ringlets flowing over her shoulders, a lavender sweater hugging the swerves of her hips, a long, straight black skirt covering equally dark boots.

Rick's stomach muscles contracted until they burned. Daisy looked like she belonged in St. Louis, looked like she should've been strolling city sidewalks instead of kicking around a place mired in tradition—a place like Kane's Crossing, where they made great efforts to celebrate the past, not the future.

Hell. Rick couldn't offer her a future, either. Not the kind a woman like Daisy deserved.

She scanned the room, her gaze stopping on him. When Daisy smiled, it was as if a spotlight flared around her, making her the only focal point in a dark world.

He couldn't believe that smile was for him, a guy standing in a shaded corner, avoiding everyone as strenuously as they avoided him.

But wasn't that what he'd wanted since coming back to his country from the Gulf? To be left alone?

He could feel his boots unglue themselves from their stubborn spot on the floor, could feel himself stepping into the light just to get close to her again.

Then, with a jarring pop, the moment burst open.

The three biggest troublemakers in the town—Sonny Jenks, Junior Crabbe and the dust-devil otherwise known as Madcap Mitzi Antle—crashed through the door, brushing by Daisy with their donkey-bray laughter and grease-worn T-shirts.

"Let's get the party going!" yelped Mitzi, shoving her baseball cap back on her ponytailed head.

In truth, it seemed as if they'd started the festivities about an hour ago. The threesome weaved through the crowd, bumping into members of the town council and farmers alike.

Daisy merely tilted her head at Rick, sauntering over to him with a saucy lift of the eyebrow. When she reached him, she was careful to leave a respectable space between their bodies.

So much for thinking that she'd flaunt their relationship in front of the town.

"What's a guy like you doing in a place like this?" she asked, grinning.

Pillowy-soft skin. Meadow-fresh perfume. Wet-hot kisses.

Couldn't he think of anything else?

He tried to seem unaffected, miles away from losing himself in her charm. "I thought I'd see how foolish this town could get. Isn't this what would happen if you crossed *Hee Haw* with *Twin Peaks*?"

The mayor's voice still rang over the hall, not that anyone was paying attention. In fact, the noise level had intensified during the last few minutes, especially with the entrance of Sonny, Junior and Mitzi.

Daisy scanned the room again, then stood on tiptoe to speak in his ear, tingling his skin with her warm breath.

"I'm nervous."

He merely glanced at her, almost afraid to ask why.

As she continued, Daisy plucked at the hem of her sweater. "Coral tells me that Peter's coming back into town tonight from his top-secret business."

They didn't really talk about Tarkin much. It was too sharp a reminder of real life. And he was glad they didn't discuss him. Their time together was too sacred, a time when they could forget about everything else except the present.

Daisy stopped her fidgeting, smoothing down her sweater. "He's going to know that I've moved out. And Coral, darn her, is still there in his house. She refuses to move."

"Well, dammit, Daisy," he said. "Tell her you're not marrying the man."

She flattened her hands over her stomach, wide-eyed. He hadn't meant to speak so harshly, hadn't meant to hurt her in any way.

"I have told her," she said. "You know that."

Rick didn't want to talk about it, but before he could say anything, old Deacon Chaney, owner of the town's drug store, whizzed by them.

"Have mercy on me, woman!" he yelled over his shoulder.

Thank God, thought Rick. A distraction, just when he needed one.

Daisy moved out of Deacon's way, coming chest

to chest with Rick. He held her there, coveting her warmth, her body.

Out of the corner of his gaze, Rick saw Mrs. Spindlebund—the town crier, the woman who'd blown Daisy's St. Louis cover—scuttle by.

"Come 'ere, Deacon Chaney, you rascal," she said, slurring her usually crisp words. "I aim to have a kiss."

Rick couldn't believe his ears. He couldn't do anything more than shoot a glance at Daisy.

"I heard it, too," she said. "We must be in hell."

By now, the room was fairly swirling with activity, almost as if the town was drunk with energy. The mayor had finished presenting awards, leaving the mike open.

Unfortunately, Sonny Jenks took the opportunity to park himself in front of the crowd, shushing them with an ear-splitting, "Hesh up, now!"

The room fell silent, except for the distraction of a few teenage giggles.

Sonny whipped off his baseball cap and fell to one knee, dipping the mike stand to accommodate this feat. "I got a burnin' heart, my friends."

A high-school jock yelled from the rafters. "It's the punch, Sonny!"

All the other kids laughed wildly, starting to chant, "Spike! Spike! Spike!"

Sonny shushed them again. "I'm sayin' what's in my soul. Mitzi Antle, let's get ourselves married."

Silence.

Then a laugh from the refreshment table. Mitzi was

back there, holding up a drained cup, clutching her belly while doubled over giggling.

Junior Crabbe rushed the stage, grabbing the mike. "Don't do it, Mitzi. I got the love for you, too, honey."

Suddenly, voices exploded, filling the air like confetti from a burst party favor. The room vibrated with chaos as the kids continued their "Spike!" chant. Then, to make matters worse, Mrs. Spindlebund seized the microphone and started singing—well, actually, screaming—a love song to Deacon Chaney.

The mayor liberated the microphone and its stand, putting it on the floor on the stage's right side. Mrs. Spindlebund continued her serenade, unfazed.

Throughout all this, Rick felt Daisy watching him, and he knew it was because he hadn't commented on Tarkin's return home. Daisy would have to confront her ex-fiancé now, and that would change the tone between her and Rick—for the worse.

It'd make their relationship more serious.

But now, a question still lingered on her lips; he could tell.

Would he give her enough strength to leave her old promises behind?

The mayor tapped his foot as Sheriff Sam Reno took the stage. His presence alone hushed the crowd.

Without a mike, he said, "We've gotten rid of that spiked punch, ladies and gentlemen. Now, I will be taking people in for being drunk in public, especially if you're underage." Here, there was an adolescent rush for the doors. "And there're deputies outside by the cars, just to see that there's no drinking and driving."

Sam nodded to the crowd. "I regret having to see some of what went on up here. In spite of those lasting images, folks, have a good night."

He deserted the stage, leaving the hall tensed with penitence.

At that moment, as people exited the party, Peter Tarkin entered, bodies parting as if he had the power to separate the sea. Dressed in his suit, he was all business. Rick couldn't imagine what Daisy had been thinking to almost marry the guy. It would've been a grand waste.

Daisy spotted him, too, as Tarkin strolled toward the stage. "Just look at him. See how he's preening in front of the Spencers? He's scared to death that they'll reclaim their place in society."

Her tone was a far cry from the unsure whispers of her wedding day, when she'd torn into Meg's bakery and asked to hide behind the counter. A measure of pride made his chest ache.

"I'm going to get this over with," she said, starting to walk toward him.

"Daisy. Now?"

"I can't stand this anymore. I can make a clean break if I know you're here watching me. Supporting me."

God, she was gazing at him as if he was her savior, the man who'd do anything to rescue her.

He couldn't stop the words from rushing out. "And

what're you going to want afterward, Daisy? What do you think I can give you?''

Her eyes were so blue, so innocent. She hadn't seen what he had as a nineteen-year-old. She hadn't had to deal with the consequences of being someone's protector.

She said, ''I thought you could give me... I was hoping...''

''Don't say it.'' He started walking toward the emergency exit by the stage, a space devoid of people, a black hole that would allow him to escape.

She followed him, still talking, leaving the remaining partygoers staring at what she was saying. ''Why don't you let me in, Rick?''

He stopped, turned to face her. ''Listen, if you're out to make me a better man, forget it. I'm beyond the 'love conquers all' garbage that normal people use to comfort themselves. Love can't solve everything.''

Her voice lowered. ''And sex can?''

It had so far.

But he couldn't bring himself to tell her that. ''Don't ask for more than we have now, Daisy.''

Her lower lip trembled, a prelude to something Rick couldn't handle. This conversation was too close to feeling, too close to caring.

He cursed, then made his way toward the stage exit.

Daisy caught up with him, latching on to his sleeve, whipping him around with a surprising strength.

''But I love you,'' she said.

Her voice seemed to echo through the hall. Seconds

later, after the initial shock of hearing her say the dreaded words aloud, Rick saw the reason her sentiments had been amplified.

They were standing next to the live microphone.

And next to Peter Tarkin.

Daisy didn't care anymore.

Any other person would've wanted to dig themselves a hole to hide in after shouting their love to the world—and to a man who couldn't give a rat's hind end.

But, no, not Daisy Cox. She wanted to stand here, between the man the town thought she'd be marrying and the man who didn't want her at all.

She could tell he didn't return her affections by the way he closed himself off, his gaze extinguished of the fire she'd seen when they'd made love this past week, his shoulders squared to support the wall that had surrounded him once again.

Even as her voice still bounced off the rafters, even as the audience stared at her with their mouths agape, Daisy wouldn't take back her proclamation.

No more lies.

She was faintly aware of Peter commandeering the mike, starting the damage control. "I love you, too, honey," he said into the microphone, pretending her words had been addressed to him. Several "aaahs" issued from the crowd but, to Daisy, it was merely background noise.

"Rick?" she whispered, hoping he'd say something and, at the same time, dreading his answer. Or lack of an answer.

Time seemed to roar over her head, poised like a storm cloud.

Then, without even a change of expression, Rick spoke softly. "I can't love you, Daisy." And, with that, he disappeared in the darkness of the exit.

She couldn't move. Not with this cold fist of reality wrapped around her throat. Not with the slap of what he'd said ringing in her ears.

Was it possible to live without breathing? Because she was clawing for oxygen and couldn't get any. The room became a blur of colors, Peter's voice and nausea.

A pair of arms caught Daisy before she sank into a heap on the floor. Coral's voice sounded in her ear.

"Let's get you home, Dizzy," she said, sounding once again like the mother Daisy hadn't known.

She needed that comfort now, at her lowest moment. Needed to know that there was someone who loved her.

And that someone was her sister, not Rick Shane.

Chapter Fourteen

Coral got Daisy home before she could make a further fool of herself.

After Coral had directed the maid to whip up some warm milk and a snack, she had taken Daisy to her old bedroom, where she'd made sure her younger sister was comfortable.

But how could Daisy rest when she felt sick to her stomach? Her whole body felt frozen with rejection.

"Peter's going to be here soon," Coral said, without a trace of scolding.

"I know. On a scale of one to ten, how bad was I?"

Coral's skin grew mottled. "It was a three thousand on the charts."

"Oh, God."

"Don't worry. Peter had the situation in hand. He has everyone believing that you were professing your great devotion to him. Remember, you weren't up on stage for everyone to see. Nobody was really even paying attention before your voice came on the mike. Then, Peter acted quickly. You'll avoid a scandal, I should think."

Daisy took a sip of milk, feeling light-headed when the soothing liquid slipped down her throat. When she tried to speak, her words were barely audible. "I'm so in love with Rick, Coral. But there's no chance of him loving me back."

"Déjà vu." Coral took a seat on the bed. "This is exactly what happened when you fell in love with that kid when you were seventeen. Then, it was bye-bye Miss America. Now, it's—"

"Not the same." Pain had settled as a dull throb around her heart. "I love Rick with all my soul."

Coral watched her, as if deciding something.

"What?" asked Daisy.

Her sister paused. "Nothing. Listen, Peter's going to be livid. He knows that you moved out, and now this...."

It was on the tip of Daisy's tongue to say, *I'm not going to marry him, Coral. Get it out of your head.*

But then she realized that there was nothing else waiting for her. No one else who wanted her more than Peter did.

Who cared anymore? Rick didn't love her.

The front door crashed shut. Daisy waited to hear

the thud of shoes on the carpet in front of her old bedroom.

"I want to talk to Peter on my own," she said.

Coral shook her head. "No, Daisy, I'm here for you."

She always had been. Daisy recalled images from her childhood: Coral coming home from a house-cleaning job, smelling like cleanser, grit caked in the lines of her hands. Coral at one of Daisy's pageants, slumped in her chair, asleep because she'd worked sixteen hours straight that day. Coral snapping off the car radio as a newscast talked about the case of a famous convict.

She'd wanted to be a prosecutor, then maybe go into civil practice. But having to take care of Daisy had killed those dreams.

Daisy owed her. Big time.

Without preamble, Peter jammed through the door, his tie askew, his hair mussed. "What the devil is going on?"

Setting down her milk on the night table, Daisy folded her hands over a knee. Coral jumped up from the bed, hovering at her sister's back.

Daisy couldn't even bring herself to comment on Peter's frustration. A few days ago, she would've felt that he'd gotten his just desserts. Now, it didn't really matter.

She said, "Is the town having a field day, Peter? Or did you exact a little spin doctoring at the hall?"

Peter must have realized that he looked flustered because, with the utmost control, he used a trembling hand to straighten his tie, to slick back his hair. "To-morrow's newspaper will mention your impromptu declaration of love *for me*. It'll also explain the mysterious 'love juice' in the punch, just to add credence to the gesture."

Daisy shook her head. "You are a master."

"You're right," he said, a small smile curving his mouth. "Embarrassment is not on my agenda."

With a deep breath of fortitude, Daisy turned around to glance at Coral. Her sister shook her head, indicating that she wasn't leaving the room. Odd. It was almost as if Coral didn't want her alone with Peter.

Well, she wasn't in a fighting mood. Let Coral stay if she wanted to.

Daisy gestured toward a chair, and Peter took her meaning and sat in it, stretching one leg over the other as he composed himself.

When he was settled, Daisy said, "You might have caught on to the fact that I'm not in love with you, Peter. I never have been. Never will be, either."

Words. Cold, steely words.

Funny how they could break your heart even though they couldn't touch you.

A sob knifed through her chest as she remembered what Rick had told her tonight. *I can't love you.*

She held back the tears, noting how Peter hadn't even shifted in his chair.

"Daisy," he said, his voice as smooth as a stroke of oil paint smeared across a canvas. "You're a smart girl, a pretty girl. Haven't you always known that love wasn't what I wanted from you?''

She paused. Actually, she *had* always known that Peter lacked passion for her. That had become especially apparent after she'd met Rick and experienced all-consuming desire firsthand.

What was it about her that people couldn't love?

Was it because she'd turned into a plump travesty of the ideal woman? Or was it because she wasn't meant to find that one great love of her life?

Maybe happily ever after just wasn't in the cards for her.

Daisy smiled frostily at Peter, conveying that she'd always known his intentions. She was to have been a business wife. Nothing more.

He leaned forward in his chair, and Daisy could detect the spark of excitement in his gaze. A flash of Peter's corporate wheeler-dealer side.

''Image is everything. One day, I'm going to own everything the eye can see from this window.''

He flicked his fingers toward the curtains, but she didn't look. Rick's rejection had shut her down, sapped her of energy.

Without a hitch, he continued. ''I'll need you next to me. You're a business partner, closing deals and making my associates feel as if they're working with a classy liaison. My own golden Miss Spencer County, polished by manners and Southern charm.''

She couldn't even bring herself to still feel offended. Rick wasn't going to be in her life anymore. Why did Peter's plans matter?

With Rick, she could've spent her nights in his bed, pressed against the length of his muscles, moving with his every thrust as she whispered her love into his ear. She could've lived in his isolated cabin, feeding off the way he looked at her with that hunger in his dark eyes. She could've flown with him, traveling the sky to places she'd only dreamed about.

But those were fantasies. Hopes that'd been shattered tonight by his blunt words.

I can't love you.

Daisy narrowed her eyes at Peter, shifting into a personality she hadn't known existed. "So I'm still part of your ultimate plan? You still want to marry me?"

He nodded and, for once, Daisy felt that he was taking her seriously. She had something he wanted, and her head swam with the dizzy realization of power.

She'd never had control of her life before this moment. Coral had governed her, and so had bulimia. But now Daisy was at the steering wheel.

Maybe she would have enjoyed the feeling if it wasn't so damned empty.

"All right, Peter," she said. "I've got a few needs to be met."

He laughed in obvious disbelief, but his mirth faded as he realized she was earnest. "What are they?"

Coral placed a hand on Daisy's shoulder. "You don't have to do this."

Both Daisy and Peter shot her sister a glance, and Coral grew silent, jaw tensed.

"First," said Daisy, "we'll have separate bedrooms, and you won't be invited to come into mine."

Peter's smug grin answered her. What did he care? He'd sleep with women like Liza Cochrane again, and Daisy knew it.

The thought was actually a big relief.

"Next," she said, "you lay off about my weight. If I want to lose some pounds, I'll do it in my own time. I have it on good authority that I look pretty decent just the way I am." The image of Rick reclining on the bed and saying she was beautiful cut into her. Then, with a lift of her head, she recovered. "Got it?"

She could hear Coral's sharp inhalation of breath, could see Peter raise his eyebrows.

"I'm sure you care about your appearance," he said.

Daisy crossed her arms, daring him to tell her that she was too chubby, too unappealing to lead dinner parties and social events.

Maybe he knew that she wasn't going to take any more guff from him, so he clipped a quick nod, then said, "Now, my conditions. I want children."

Daisy's stomach flipped. She wanted kids, too. Rick's kids.

Tears gathered in her eyes, but she fought them. "We'll say that I can't have babies. I'm sure we'll gain a lot of sympathy when we adopt sons and daughters from the Reno Center."

For a moment, Daisy didn't know if he'd go for her plan, but he obviously realized that she wouldn't be pushed around anymore.

He gave her a glance that clearly indicated that he thought he could change her mind, then stood, giving his pants a quick swipe to erase the wrinkles. "No matter the cost, I want that wedding to happen soon. Consult with the planner and let me know when it'll happen. I'll arrange to be in town."

"How kind," said Daisy.

She got to her feet, too, and held out her hand for him to shake it.

For a moment, she thought he'd refuse. Then he grasped her fingers, a gleam of something that Daisy thought might be respect in his eyes.

Afterward, he left the room, and Daisy sighed in relief. At the same time, she didn't feel any better about herself, couldn't shake the suspicion that she was exacting revenge on Rick by doing the one thing he'd tried to save her from.

Marrying Peter Tarkin.

Coral stepped in front of her, face ashen. "What did you just do, Dizzy?"

"I thought you'd be happy about this. After all, you haven't even moved out of his house."

God, she sounded like an automaton, programmed without emotion, wired for efficiency and results.

"You're going to have to trust me about living here," said Coral, drawing Daisy into a hug. "I'll explain later. All the same, you might want to rethink this devil's deal."

Why? thought Daisy. Rick didn't want her. She might as well be married to the man who'd loaned them money, might as well pay off that debt.

Daisy tried to muster up enough strength to embrace her sister right back, but she failed. Instead, she merely leaned her head on Coral's shoulder, her gaze fixed on the window, her mind floating up to the sky on the wings of times past.

"I'm going to do the right thing," she said. "I'm going to take care of you now, Coral."

Though she tried hard to not feel a thing, Daisy couldn't escape the heat of her sister's tears as they bathed her cheek.

Daisy didn't dare give in to the threat of her own.

By the next day, news of the second wedding was on the tip of every tongue. Including Matt Shane's.

He stood in Rick's cabin, watching his brother use a rag to wipe the grease from a wrench that he'd plucked from a toolbox on the floor.

Rick glanced at him. "What'd you just say?"

His cowboy-booted sibling shuffled and avoided Rick's gaze. "Daisy Cox is marrying that son-of-a-gun next weekend. Hey, you know, I thought you and her were…"

The announcement bounced around Rick's mind like a ricocheting bullet. The damage from the news bled down over his eyes, making him see red.

He pitched the wrench across the room, watching it crash into a wall, where it left a jagged scar. The action didn't make him feel any better, dammit. He looked for something else to throw.

"Hey," said Matt, advancing on him with his hands spread out. He resembled a hostage negotiator, trying to calm a man with a smoking gun. "Don't bring down the house."

Rick's arm swooped out to clear a nearby table of its papers and pens. He'd dismantle every piece of wood with his bared teeth if he damn well pleased.

This was his fault. He'd told Daisy that he couldn't love her, and he'd regretted the sentiment the second it'd left his mouth.

Her face had fallen, and her eyes had dimmed. The way she'd looked at him had almost torn out his heart. But it was for the best, he kept telling himself.

However, sending her back into Tarkin's grip hadn't been his intention.

"Listen," said Matt, patting him on the back and leading him to an area where there was nothing to throw. "I don't know what happened between the two of you, but you're gonna blow a gasket if you keep this up."

The weight of his brother's hand on his back actually calmed Rick somewhat. He thought he'd never see the day when he welcomed Matt's efforts to help.

Matt must have known what Rick was thinking. "I may not have been there for you in the past, but I am now."

That's right. He'd changed from the arrogant old Matthew to the new Matt, a man Rick was actually starting to like a little. It took guts to step up and apologize for past mistakes.

Not that Rick could do the same, himself. Or could he? What was so hard about it anyway?

He blew out a breath, girding himself to wander into unknown territory here. "Jeez, Matt. I blew it last night."

"How?"

This was the tough part. "I told Daisy I couldn't ever love her."

Silence.

Rick chanced a glance at his big brother. Matt's brows drew together in a line, almost like a fill-in-the-blank where Rick could've written a term like "idiot" or "peckerwood."

"Why can't you love her?" he asked. "Loving's pretty easy, once you get the hang of it."

He felt himself start to shrug, then realized that the laconic gesture was part of the problem. He did care. Too much. "I…"

Good God, he couldn't even tell his own brother about the Gulf, about Clarice and the aftermath of her death. "I'm afraid that when Daisy finds out what I'm really like, she's gonna hate me."

There. That was most of it.

Matt shook his head, rolling his eyes. "And that's all he wrote."

Rick must've seemed baffled, because Matt took one look at him and continued.

"I'm gonna give you years worth of advice in

about five minutes flat, okay? So don't tell me I never made anything up to you.''

Advice? Yeah, maybe that was what he needed to stop the trembling in his veins, the impotent anger surging through every pulse of his blood.

Matt leaned against the couch. ''Women like to take care of their men. If you've got some kind of dark spot on your soul, Daisy seems like the kind of girl who'll want to shed some light on it, to save you from your problems. They love it when they can make a new man out of you.''

Make a man out of him.

Before Rick had gone off to war, Matt had told him not to come back until he'd achieved manhood. Well, it'd happened, in a moment splattered with blood and guilt.

If Rick told Daisy about the remorse that had crept under his skin ever since he'd left the country, would she really redeem him?

Right. He couldn't even forgive himself for what he'd done, so what made him think Daisy would do it?

Rick smiled, and it weighed on him like the drag of an embedded bullet. ''You can't make a new man out of a guy who's lost his humanity.''

Matt lowered his voice. ''I remember when you came to Dad's funeral, Rick. Nobody had seen you since you'd left for the war. And when you returned home…'' He shook his head. ''We didn't know who you were anymore. You came back a different person.''

"Hell, Matt. I left as a boy, and you dared me to grow up while I was gone. I did change. So why're you complaining?"

Matt didn't answer, probably because there was no calm way of countering Rick's vitriol.

After a shattered second, his brother stood straight, looking Rick in the eye. "I'm just glad to have you back."

Rick swallowed, nodded. Matt gave an embarrassed laugh, swinging his arm around Rick in an awkward, heartfelt embrace.

"Don't be stupid," said Matt, as Rick broke the contact. "Don't let that girl go."

Rick watched as his brother left the cabin, watched his headlights cut the falling night, then fade to black.

Don't let her go.

He sauntered over to his chest of drawers, opened the top one and ran a finger over Daisy's wedding tiara.

As Rick held up the crown, he thought that the gems sparkled like her eyes on the night they'd danced in the St. Louis jazz club.

He set the object down on top of the chest, then reached inside the drawers once again, this time holding his Silver Star medal.

Its five points nestled against his palm. He'd forgotten how the red-white-and-blue ribbon could strike a patriotic note in his heart, how the silver in the midst of gold could gleam like a nighttime wish.

What if he did tell Daisy about the Gulf? What if,

in the face of his confession, she did back away with horror etched on her face?

God, did he really want to take this chance? Having her hate him for not being able to love seemed so much easier than having her hate him for what he'd done to make him hide in a cabin for a good chunk of his life.

Daisy Cox is marrying that son-of-a-gun next weekend.

He picked up the tiara again, absorbing the sight of it. Then, with an oath, he heaved it to the ground. It shattered into a thousand tiny stars, each blinking up at him with the dullness of dead hope.

The evening before Daisy's second wedding day, Rick slumped on his couch, an empty beer bottle dangling from his fingers as he watched flames from the fire spitting at him.

A knock sounded at his door. Rick lifted the bottle to his lips and tilted back his head, feeling the last drop of brew wiggle over the stubble of his chin.

Well, damn it all. He'd drunk all of his provisions.

When he'd woken up this morning, realizing that Daisy would probably be partying away at her bachelorette shindig tonight, he'd started his beer odyssey. Who knew that a marathon of brew wouldn't be enough to keep him numb?

Another knock busted at his brain.

He retaliated with a few choice phrases and hoped that the intruder would be miffed enough to leave.

No such luck.

The door opened, spiriting in two different sets of footsteps. Both intruders stopped right in front of Rick.

Matt shifted a thumb toward the door. "That's what you get for not locking the thing."

Sam Reno stood next to Rick's brother, his sheriff's badge glinting with reflections of the twilight. "Isn't this a stinking mess? By God, Rick. Were you drinking the beer or showering in it?"

Rick absently stuck his fingertip in the bottle's opening, listening to the *pop* as he wrenched it free again. "Who invited you all?"

"Consider your party crashed, Rick." Sam kicked at the glass on the floor, where Rick had flung the bottles, hardly caring if they broke or not. "Matt, you didn't tell me he'd be zonked out of his gourd."

"He's been like this all week, but I thought he'd come around."

Matt caught himself, as if he was reluctant to step back into the role of bossy big brother. Problem was, Rick would've welcomed some butt-kicking right about now, not that he'd admit it.

He continued staring at the fire, hard pressed to let the other guys know how much he hated himself for being unable to come clean with Daisy.

Sam obviously didn't suffer from the big brother syndrome. He kicked Rick's boot, making him scowl in the sheriff's direction.

"You're giving men a bad name," Sam said. "Get your rear in gear."

Rick actually chuffed. "Give me a good reason."

"Because you've got a chance to win back your woman."

At this, Rick froze, his mind clearing a little. He sat straighter, warier. "What makes you so sure that I want Daisy back?"

Matt chuckled. "Hey, you stubborn flyboy. Don't fool a couple of fools. We had to swallow some pride when it came to winning back our own wives. Right, Sam?"

The sheriff grinned. "I did enjoy eating some fine crow before I admitted my feelings for Ashlyn."

Rick could almost feel Daisy's heart beating against his chest, could almost feel her hair woven through his fingers. What if he could hold her again? What if he could tell her he loved her?

Oh, God. He did, didn't he? That's why he hadn't been able to function this week. The loss of her had hit him harder than he'd thought possible.

He was in love with the woman.

A sense of relief swept over him. He'd admitted it to himself, and that was half the battle. Right?

Wrong. That was only the beginning.

"What makes you think she'd want anything to do with me?" he asked, just to test the waters.

Both Matt and Sam laughed. Matt said, "According to the women, they've never seen a more morose bride. Rachel said that when Daisy was in Darla's Beauty Shop the other day, Daisy looked about ready to cry."

Crying. Hmmm. It wasn't that Rick liked to see her sad, but the image offered a little hope.

But, then again, what did he think? That she'd stopped loving him in the space of a week?

Sam hunched over, taking the beer bottle away from Rick. He let it go.

"How would you like a chance to make up for all your mistakes?" he asked.

Rick's pulse was starting to race. "But—"

Matt pointed at his brother, halting the buts. "No more excuses."

He was right. Rick wouldn't think about how Daisy would react when he told her his secrets. Hell, if she couldn't love everything about him, then she wasn't the woman he was meant to be with.

It felt good to admit that.

That's it. He was finally going to stop running.

"Let's hear your plan, Sheriff," he said.

Sam became serious, all law-and-order. "Coral Cox tipped off the FBI to some very interesting information. And now we know why Peter Tarkin is so damned wealthy."

Rick leaned forward, leaving behind his beer buzz and all his doubts besides. "And?"

"And," said Matt, "you're going to have the perfect opportunity to save Daisy from a second wedding, Rick. Are you up to it?"

Was he ready? Because, this time, when he spirited Daisy away, it'd be for keeps.

Rick nodded, his body heating up at the idea of Daisy leaving Tarkin at the altar yet again.

"I think I've been ready for years," he said.

He just wondered if Daisy would be.

Chapter Fifteen

Hopefully, she'd do it right this time.

The long-sleeved wedding dress fit just fine for an off-the-rack speed replacement, the orchids decorating the church were fresh and creative, and the bridesmaids—sans Liza Cochrane, of course—were wearing the same dresses from the first matrimonial attempt.

For a last-minute event, the wedding planner had pulled off a miracle. As Daisy stood before the preacher, she could take pride in at least that much.

For the millionth time this week, she repeated her new mantra: *I'm in control of my life now. I'm doing the right thing by marrying Peter Tarkin.*

The stem of her bouquet bit into her skin as she clutched it.

As if from the haze of a bad dream, the preacher's voice floated over her. He was talking about love again, so she shut out the words, knowing they'd hurt too much if she listened.

She could feel Peter's heavy gaze on her. He'd returned to town yesterday, after another sudden business trip, just in time to exchange vows. Part of her had been hoping that he'd miss the ceremony. But no such luck.

While the preacher droned on, the guests stirred in their seats, causing Daisy's attention to wander. Subtly, she sneaked a glance behind her, to see what the ruckus was.

Sheriff Reno and Ashlyn, who wore a huge grin in addition to her rainbow-hued skirt and sweater, leaned against the back wall of the church, cuddling one of their Maltese dogs under each arm. Two men in dark suits and ties flanked Sam, his wife and the pups. If Daisy didn't know better, she'd say that the two strangers had stepped out of a *Men in Black* movie, with their stoic demeanors and ramrod postures.

Next to her, Peter stiffened, then ignored the intrusion as his best man stepped forward with Daisy's wedding ring. When Coral followed suit with Peter's piece of jewelry, Daisy caught her eye.

Like Ashlyn, her sister was smiling, cheeks flushed in a way that sent goose pimples over Daisy's skin.

The preacher snapped her back to attention. "Do you, Daisy Rae Cox, take this man to be your lawful wedded husband, to have and to hold from this day forward?"

To have and to hold? What a joke.

A voice from the seats behind her stopped Daisy's response.

"Well, I never," said Mrs. Spindlebund.

Ashlyn's voice carried from the back of the church. "You sure tried with Deacon Chaney!"

As the entire crowd tittered, Daisy faced the guests, curious about what had caused Mrs. Spindlebund's declaration. The elderly gossip slipped down several inches in her seat, encouraging more laughter.

Then Daisy saw what the fuss was about. She gasped, hardly believing it.

Rick Shane sauntered purposefully down the aisle, wearing his usual black clothing and an equally dark expression. The serious strangers and Sam Reno followed in his wake, bearing down on her.

A rolling tremble roared through her body, and she dropped the bouquet, holding her hands in front of her as if to ward off Rick.

"Hey, Daisy," he said, right before bending, latching an arm around the back of her knees and then scooping her body over his shoulder.

The motion seemed to stretch for an hour, and she was keenly aware of her taffeta dress rustling over the sound of the guests' *ooooo*'s of surprise. Aware of the red aisle carpet rushing up to greet her as she plunked over Rick's shoulder like a sack of horse feed.

He whirled her around, intending to exit the church, using the aisle that she should've been marching down with Peter as man and wife. Still stunned, she glanced up as the men in black approached her wide-eyed groom and said, ''Peter Tarkin, we've got a warrant for your arrest for the unlawful transport of stolen art over state lines.''

The world was bouncing with every step Rick took. As the altar receded, Daisy fixated on Coral, who was watching Peter's mortification with a smile on her face. Then Coral turned to Daisy, wiggling her fingers in a smug little wave.

Reality hit Daisy with the force of a karate kick.

She was on Rick Shane's back, being carried away from a wedding she'd actually agreed to.

As the openmouthed guests became a blur, Daisy heard the church door bang open when Rick burst through it.

She pounded on his back. ''Hey! What are you doing? Did you receive an invitation? I don't think so.''

He just laughed, going about the business of crossing the parking lot.

The blacktop stared Daisy in the face. She attempted to shimmy off Rick's shoulder, but that maneuver only succeeded in him clamping a hand over her rear end.

She could almost see him smiling because he'd copped a feel, the jerk.

''You're crazy, you know that, Rick Shane? First you tell me you can't love me, then here you are ruining my wedding. And, by the way, I *wanted* to get married this time.''

No she didn't. But she wanted Rick to think that she was unaffected by his treatment of her.

Liar, liar.

She heard his Jeep door opening and couldn't resist wiggling around a bit more, just to make his mission difficult. He was going to win this round, no doubt about it. Going back to Peter was out of the question, especially since he was being arrested.

Especially since she hadn't *really* wanted to get hitched to him.

Rick slapped her on the derriere and deposited her in the passenger seat. As he shut the door, Daisy crossed her arms over her chest, jutting out her jaw in a show of defiance.

She'd wait until he sat down, then she'd really give it to him.

As soon as he entered the vehicle, he started the engine. The efficiency almost impressed Daisy, but not quite.

"You think I'm going somewhere with you?" she asked.

"I believe so." He grinned, then pressed pedal to the metal, taking off in a screech of burned rubber.

"Not for long." As she sped up, she fixed her safety belt around her. "When we stop, I'm jumping out of this wheezing contraption, and I'm hoofing it to the nearest pay phone to call the—"

"You might've noticed that the sheriff was a part of this grand scheme. Any other ideas?"

During the ensuing pause, Rick took the time to see that Daisy had indeed buckled herself in and was riding comfortably. He was kind of enjoying this, reliving the sight of Daisy crashing into the bakery in her first wedding dress, then taking off to St. Louis to fall in love.

He was ready to come clean, to finish what they'd started in that hotel room when she'd asked him why he'd stopped making love to her.

Out of the corner of his eye, he saw Daisy toss up her hands in apparent surrender. She said, "So Peter was being arrested, huh?"

He speared her a glance, taking in the spray of white flowers holding back her curls. She hadn't worn a veil this time, and he wondered if that had been on purpose, to change the tone of this wedding, to make it more successful than the first one.

"Coral really stuck it to Tarkin," said Rick, unable to hide the satisfaction in his voice. Back at the church, justice was being served on a silver spoon to a most deserving customer. "After you came back from St. Louis, she realized that the marriage was a selfish idea. Luckily, she resented your former fiancé enough to eavesdrop on his business dealings."

"No. I thought…" Daisy seemed shocked. "She was only protecting me again. When is she going to stop?"

Rick couldn't think of an answer, so he took another tack. "Coral got suspicious of all those secret, sudden business trips Tarkin was taking. She heard a strange phone call where he was talking about paying off smugglers, then connected that information to the paintings. She also caught your love muffin red-handed while he was mounting a valuable work of art behind another one in his study. Good thing he never caught your sister snooping around.''

Daisy shook her head. ''And she called the FBI. She's a frustrated lawyer, investigating a case. That's why she didn't want to leave the house. She was less accepting of Peter's demands than I thought.''

Rick gunned the Jeep up the road to his cabin, knowing that nobody would dare bother them here. Not when he was about to discover whether Daisy really loved him enough to stay.

He fought the tightness in his belly and concentrated on the moment at hand. First, he'd have to lead Daisy gently, let her know that she could trust him again.

''Tarkin made a fortune smuggling stolen art across state lines. He was playing a chancy game. It was just a matter of time before he got caught.''

''Then why did *I* get caught?'' she asked.

Right. Why had he thrown her over his shoulder and taken her away from her friends and family?

He pulled into a parking spot, cutting the engine. ''Because I'm going to be with you the rest of your life, and I wanted the rest of your life to start now.''

Daisy undid her seat belt, but didn't get out of the vehicle. ''You sure pulled a one-eighty. A week ago, you didn't want anything to do with me.''

''Yeah,'' he said, reaching out to run his finger over the line of her jaw. ''That's what I thought. Now you're going to have to decide whether you want anything to do with *me*.''

"Don't be ridiculous. It takes me a long time to fall out of love with a guy." Without looking at him, she exited the Jeep, shutting the door before he could say another word.

He watched her walk into his home, her white dress clouding over the boards of his porch like the trail following a jet in the sky.

God. The next hour would determine whether or not her love was strong enough to survive his stories. If so, he'd be the luckiest schmuck alive. If not...

Hell. If not, he'd stay as he was.

A man who belonged in a cage of his own device, punishing himself for the sins of his past.

After entering the cabin, Daisy plopped on his bed, more out of spite than anything else.

Let him fantasize about their nights together. Let him wonder if she was going to shed her wedding dress and start honeymooning with him.

True, she was being cruel. But he couldn't just saunter back into her life and expect to continue an affair in which they didn't talk to each other, in which he didn't love her as much as she loved him.

His shadow crossed the door's threshold before his body did. Then he just stood there, hands in jeans' pockets, gaze focused on the wall, seeing nothing.

He reminded her of a statue she'd seen in Washington, D.C., when she'd traveled there as a spokesmodel. At the Vietnam Memorial.

Three soldiers had stood, frozen in time, their sights fixed on the wall with that ghostly, ten-yard stare. They'd looked so young, too tender to be sent away to shed blood for their country.

The whole experience of the Wall had broken Daisy's heart, just like the sight of Rick right now.

He jerked out of his reverie, covering the moment by doffing his bomber jacket and tossing it on the couch. "I'm not very good at being emotional."

No kidding. But now wasn't the time for sarcasm or flip comments. His whole bearing had changed since he'd driven her away from the church. Where he used to be cocky, now he was withdrawn.

"Here's the thing, Rick." She sat up on the bed, recognizing the weight of the moment. "I'm pretty proud of myself. I've stopped avoiding my problems, and I don't intend to start running from them again. I can't be with a man who won't do the same."

"I know," he said. "I'm trying to work up the nerve to do what you did—to stop being chased by whatever's eating at me."

And that struggle was evident by the clenching of his hands into fists, by the shadow of stubble on his tightened jaw.

He took a breath, then started to pace the room slowly, like an animal circling the inside of a cage, trying to scope a way out.

Daisy kept her silence, reluctant to interrupt him.

He turned to her, lifting a finger. "Just do me a favor, okay? After I'm done talking, don't say a word."

He backtracked, retrieving his keys from his jacket, then tossed them on the bed, right next to her. "If you feel the need, all you have to do is walk out that door and never come back. I'll understand if you do that.''

Daisy was getting worried. ''Why do you think I'm going to react badly to what you have to say?''

''Because I know how I feel about myself, and I can predict how you'll feel, too.''

Suddenly, Daisy understood. ''You've never talked to anyone about what's bothering you. Have you?''

He didn't say anything. Instead, he sat on the edge of his couch, focusing on the ashes in the fireplace.

''I'm not even sure where to start.''

She knew how he felt about revealing something ugly about your past. When she'd told him about her bulimia struggle, she'd just been waiting for him to back away from her, to get that repulsed look in his eyes, to say, ''God, you're disgusting.''

But he hadn't done that.

''Start with Clarice,'' she said.

He flinched. ''Why not. Yeah. Why the hell not.''

It was as if an alternate, invisible reality had settled around him, making Rick sit straighter, making his voice more of a low bark than a whisper.

''I had a falling out with my dad and brother when I graduated, so in short order, I went into the army, pretty much to tick off the old man, but mostly to prove to Matthew that I could grow up and make something of myself.

''I knew the army would tell me what to do, would structure my life. Even if I was a goof-off in high school, I liked the thought of belonging, of being told what my place in the group was.''

She could imagine Rick, getting all that thick, dark hair chopped off. Could imagine him in camouflage, weighed down by a helmet and gear. ''You were so young when you enlisted.''

''A lot of us were. Just kids, not even old enough to drink legally.'' He grinned for a second, then the happiness disappeared. ''I was real gung ho in boot camp, and I came out of it a Private First Class. A PFC. Then we got sent to the Persian Gulf.''

Television images washed over his words: desert sand caked on soldiers' smooth faces, SCUDs launching through the night sky, reporters talking about some guy named Saddam and how the Americans were kicking some major butt in the region.

Rick's words wove themselves into her pictures. ''We got to King's Five, something like a mission control out there in the middle of nowhere, and I had the chance to meet a lot of people. Some of them were helicopter pilots. And that's where everything became clear to me. I realized that I wanted to fly. Black Hawks.''

His gaze lifted to the ceiling, eyes glazed, as if he could see the choppers hovering there. ''They're almost a thing of beauty in the air, kind of like a spider gliding across a web toward its prey. Almost unstoppable. I could see myself at the controls, veering over the land, swooping down and sweeping back up into the sky...''

A curse stopped his description.

"Go on," said Daisy. She could see the scared teenager below the surface of his skin, could see how hard he was trying to hide the vulnerability. Knowing that he carried such a soft side made her sore around the heart.

Rick blew out a breath. "After this whole Gulf thing, I was going to get back stateside and enroll in Warrant Officer Candidate School to be a pilot. I finally knew what I wanted out of life."

"Why didn't you?"

She almost wished she hadn't asked. He backed against the couch, staring straight ahead, all but shutting her out.

"We'll get there, Daisy," he said softly.

"I know." She smiled at him, telling him that he could say anything, and she'd still be on his side.

But he was talking to the fireplace again, avoiding her. "In the meantime, I was just a grunt, a radio operator with a life expectancy of about seven seconds in the field. I'd goofed up some test that told the army that this is what I'd be best at. My position would be the first to be targeted because, if you're the enemy, you want to take out communications capability right off the bat.

"But, like a lot of soldiers, my unit didn't see much action. We just waited around King's Five for an assignment, watching the other units go out and come back, missions completed. But everything wasn't all that bad. I met someone there. Clarice."

The name swept through the room on a cold wave of air.

"Clarice," Daisy repeated, a little jealous that two syllables could mean so much to Rick.

He finally glanced at her, a sad smile weighing on his lips. "She reminded me of you, Daisy. The way you'd get all feisty when I teased you at school, the way you'd put me in my place with just a look. Clarice could do that, too. And she was an older woman, smarting from her jerk of an ex-husband. I hated that she was still in love with the guy. But I worshipped her. I mean, hell, I was only nineteen and didn't know any better than to realize I didn't have a shot."

"What was she?" asked Daisy. "Your commanding officer or something?"

Rick almost smiled. "She was a medic attached to our unit. They say that God loves medics, but Clarice didn't even come home from the Gulf. How does that make sense?"

Daisy couldn't answer his question. It frustrated her that she couldn't even understand why someone would go into battle, knowing that they could be killed. How did you talk yourself into that? How did you survive it?

He said, "I remember the day before she died. We'd been hanging out, watching some other grunts shoot hoops, when she sat down next to me. Her hair was like yours, blond and curly, but cut short. She talked like a man, but I never thought she was any less a woman."

Rick swallowed, then paused. "It was like she knew she was going to die. She leaned over and kissed my forehead, without ever saying a word. Then she just left me there, with my mouth hanging open. That's what I remember the most about Clarice. That stupid kiss.''

His hesitation squeezed Daisy's stomach into a nervous knot. Did he still have feelings for that woman? Was this the reason he couldn't love Daisy?

He started again before she screwed up enough courage to ask. ''That day, we were finally assigned to go out in the field, to 'take a hill' in order to advance our position in Iraq. We were so naïve, so excited to finally get it on with the other side.

''A scouting party was requested to go ahead and report back their findings. Being a radio operator, I was one of the lucky ones. A chopper dropped us off a couple of klicks away from our unit.''

Daisy felt sick, nervous. She couldn't imagine Rick anyplace but in this cabin, couldn't think of him in a foreign country, being targeted by strangers who didn't care what a good man he was.

His voice brought her back to the moment.

''Before we could report back with anything substantial, we started to take on enemy fire. Mortar explosions were going off all around us, and then came the sniper. Those bullets were snapping past our heads, real damn close. Close enough to wound a sergeant in our party. I radioed coordinates for medevac to get him, because his wound looked serious.''

Rick held up his hands, looking at them as if there was blood coating his skin. ''Right away, that sniper shot my radio, disabling it. God, wouldn't you know he missed *me* all together, but that radio was toast.

And, to make matters worse, he got the two other men in the party. That left me, alone, waiting for the med-evac unit to get their butts out to us.''

He was getting more agitated, his knee vibrating up and down as he clenched his hands over his legs. ''When the Huey came, Clarice jumped out, just in time, too, because those Iraqis mortared the chopper, blew it to smithereens. So here we were, stranded without communication, bullets hissing around us.

''Clarice went right to work on the other guys, and I tried to hold off the enemy with my guns. I thought I was such hot stuff, protecting her while she tended to the guys. Then, it happened.''

He stilled his nervous legs, leaning his head back on the couch. Daisy got up from the bed, wanting to be near him. Needing to soothe him in some way.

After she sat down, she smoothed her fingers over his forehead, as if to brush off a fever.

''I tried to save her,'' he said, ''but it was too hard. The sniper got her, and there was no chance. He hit a vein in her neck, and I can remember—''

His voice choked off, and Daisy held his head to her chest, brushing his hair. ''You don't have to tell me,'' she said. ''You can stop now.''

''No.'' He spoke into the folds of her wedding dress. ''I need you to know.''

''All right. I'm here. Okay?'' She kissed his head, closing her eyes. ''I'm here.''

''I couldn't help her,'' said Rick, voice scratchy. ''I was a dumb kid who didn't know anything. There were beads of blood on her hair, and I remember how they looked like a ruby crown. It was a strange thing to think in that situation. I mean, she was *dying*. But the sight of her tore me up inside, it made me angrier than I've ever been. I couldn't even see ahead of me. But I controlled that coldness because I wanted to get the bastards who'd killed Clarice. I wanted to get to a radio for medevac to clear away the bodies of my friends. Leaving them out there was never an option.''

Daisy felt the breath leave her, almost as if Rick was going to risk his life just by telling her what happened.

He said, ''The other guys had died. I hadn't even been hit. It was almost laughable, how something had decided that the biggest idiot-kid in the party would be the one to survive. Then I started to hear Matthew's voice. 'Come back a man,' he'd said. And I would. I'd get the Iraqis back for killing the guys beside me, for murdering Clarice. I'd make them pay.

''You're trained to kill when you're a soldier. You spend hours shooting at targets. You do it so often that, after a while, the enemy becomes cardboard, just another sandman cleaned out of the way. I thought about all the training I'd gone through, thought about all the war stories the old timers told us.

''So I took matters into my own hands. I became a man, all right. I crawled to the enemy, hiding behind rocks, trying to blend in so I could get to their radio. Somehow I managed to pick off the guys who were mortaring us. Then, I had to take care of the sniper.''

He'd started to shake. The trembling was so intense that it seemed to dig through his body, to rake over his bones. Daisy felt helpless. What could she do for Rick? She couldn't take these memories back, couldn't understand enough to offer advice, couldn't find the strength to stop him from telling her the rest of his experience.

"I got right behind him," said Rick. "And I just stood there for a second, knowing that his life was in my hands. I must've made a sound, because he flinched. I told him to drop his weapons and turn around. He took my meaning and raised his arms. Then he smiled. The bastard *smiled,* as if he'd enjoyed killing my friends."

Rick's body went limp against Daisy. "Usually, you don't even see a soldier's face when you shoot him. But I looked into his eyes. He couldn't have been older than I was, probably even had a family like I did. He might've even loved someone like I'd loved Clarice. But he'd *smiled,* and that made all the difference between us.

"He flinched again, like he was going to grab his weapon. Or maybe that's just an excuse, because I killed him right there. I took another life, but this one felt like murder, not war."

"Oh, Rick," said Daisy, whispering.

He finally looked up at her, gauging her reaction. She tried her best to remain calm, as if his story was no big deal. But she couldn't.

She started crying, great, heaving sobs of misery. "You were just a kid," she repeated on a whisper.

His voice was level, dispassionate. "I got to their radio, tuned into one of our frequencies, gave coordinates, got a medevac unit out there to get me and the bodies back. My lieutenant congratulated me on a job well done. I earned a Silver Star medal because I was such a damned hero.''

And he'd come home to a place that couldn't possibly fathom what it was like to be shot at, what it was like to feel someone die in your arms, what it was like to have to kill another human being.

"He was the only person I'd ever killed while thinking," he said. "Imagine getting rewarded even though you couldn't save the woman you cared most about in this world, even though you'd put bullets into other human beings.''

Rick was silent, watching her. "I've got no scars on my skin. The only reason you know about this wound is because you wanted me to tell you. Now you can stay, or you can go.''

Daisy's mind spun. Rick thought he was a monster, didn't he? "Is this why you've locked yourself away from everyone? Because you think you're somehow not worthy of being human?''

"I'd say, in the scheme of things, I really haven't earned the right.''

Daisy shook her head, reaching out to cup his face in her hands. "If you were ugly inside, you wouldn't have punished yourself for something you had to do.''

"I didn't have to take such pleasure in ending his life.'' His dark eyes burned into her.

She ran a thumb over his lips. "I don't think you took any pleasure at all. I think you've lived for years and years, making sure you paid for what you perceive to be a crime.''

He glanced away again. ''All I ever wanted was to come back home a success, to make my dad proud of me.''

Rick tightened his jaw again, and Daisy realized that he was fighting tears. It made hers come all the harder, wrenching into her throat, making her voice shake.

''He would've understood, would've been happy to have you as a son. I've seen what's inside of you, Rick, and I still love you. You're beautiful to me, no matter how you judge yourself.''

A tiny rivulet escaped the corner of one eye, streaking down his face, catching in the stubble of his cheek. ''God, that's what I wanted to hear. I can't believe you still want to be with me.''

''Of course I do.'' And she'd help him deal with his darkness, even if it took all her energy. ''I'll never have your experiences, but I'll do my best to understand what you're going through. I'm going to be *your* protector now, waking you up when you have a bad dream, taking you away from what's hurting you inside. You can't be so hard on yourself. You're human.''

He seemed to let out a breath he'd been holding for years, then took her hands, kissing her knuckles. ''Thank you, God,'' he whispered. ''Daisy, I love you so much.''

He'd said it. Of all the prizes she'd won in her life—crowns, banners and trophies—this one meant the most. Compared to Rick's love, everything else was meaningless.

"Me, too," she said.

The late sun slanted through the window, shining over her white dress, reminding her that she'd almost made a huge mistake.

But, somehow, she felt she'd done right today. Done *very* right.

For the rest of the evening, they held each other, hardly daring to move, running their lips over each other's faces, memorizing every line and curve, breathing in measured time, matching their heartbeats.

Then night fell, and they crawled beneath the sheets, leaving Daisy's dress on the floor with Rick's jeans and T-shirts.

Discarding what they didn't need anymore.

Epilogue

Months Later

It was the perfect wedding.

Daisy wore her third dress in the space of a year, a shimmery powder-blue lace number that reflected the light in her eyes. As she stepped down the aisle toward Rick, candles flickered around the town hall, sending bright flutters of flame over the bride and the guests.

A nighttime ceremony. Daisy had requested it, since she thought every decision needed to be the opposite of her Peter Tarkin endeavors. Exchanging their vows in the evening, with Daisy wearing her curls loose under a dainty mantilla, boded well for them, she'd claimed.

Not that Rick cared much about luck.

While Daisy smiled at him, his sister Lacey banged out ''The Wedding March'' on the hall's piano, lending a lighthearted air to the evening. And, heaven knew, he needed that feel-good tint to his life.

Yup. All along, he'd just needed Daisy.

A couple months ago, after Tarkin had been incarcerated for his crimes, Rick had seen to it that Daisy and Coral were debt free, and that Coral could attend school again. She'd accepted his offer, promising to pay him back someday, when she was making enough money in a law practice.

But Rick didn't care about cash. His only concern was keeping Daisy as happy as she kept him.

She stopped at his side, a healthy blush on her cheeks, her figure filling out her dress with those shapely curves he loved. It was all he could do to hold himself back long enough to jump on their plane and spirit her to a honeymoon location—anywhere she wanted to go. They'd just wing it.

The preacher from a neighboring county started talking, but Rick wasn't listening. He was running his gaze over his future wife, wondering how she put up with living in their one-room cabin, how she kept loving him even when he occasionally awakened with nightmares.

They weren't as bad as before. But they still taunted him, the shadows receding more every time he woke up to find Daisy leaning over him, kissing the sweat from his brow, singing him to sleep again with that husky, blues-soft voice.

The ceremony continued, racing by in a blur until they got to the part where the preacher asked if anyone wanted to interrupt their union.

Both he and Daisy peered around, as if they expected another wedding to crash and burn. But it didn't.

All they saw were the faces of friends, relatives, loved ones, all here to celebrate their healing.

As the ceremony continued, Rick breathed a sigh of relief. Then, on impulse, he grabbed his fiancée, dipping her back until she squealed with surprise.

"Rick Shane, what are you doing?"

The guests all chuckled, filling Kane Spencer Hall with the sound of a community drawn together.

He smiled in his best flyboy fashion, and Daisy's heart melted in her eyes. His own belly burned in response.

"I'm making sure I claim the bride before she runs off," he said.

Daisy tossed away her modest bouquet, wrapping both arms around his neck. "Oh, ye of little faith."

"No," he said. "All my faith is in you, Daisy."

Then, with the slow passion of a plaintive song floating over a rolling river, he bent, heating his lips over hers, stretching their heartbeats into one drawn-out echo.

The preacher cleared his throat. "It's not time to kiss the bride yet," he said.

They both turned their heads, mouths still flushed against each other's, giving the clergyman a long glance.

Rick shrugged, then smiled against Daisy's lips, returning to the kiss, deepening it, making the room spin with stars and light.

And, as the guests began to clap, Daisy and Rick stayed that way, blocking out the world.

Blocking out everything except each other.

* * * * *

Coming soon only from

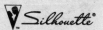

SPECIAL EDITION™

by
GINA WILKINS

After their father's betrayal, the McCloud siblings
hid their broken hearts and drifted apart.
Would one matchmaking little girl be enough
to bridge the distance...and lead them to love?

Don't miss

The Family Plan (SE #1525)
March 2003
When Nathan McCloud adopts a four-year-old, will his sexy
law partner see he's up for more than fun and games?

Conflict of Interest (SE #1531)
April 2003
Gideon McCloud wants only peace and quiet, until
unexpected visitors tempt him with the family of his dreams.

and

Faith, Hope and Family (SE #1538)
May 2003
When Deborah McCloud returns home, will she find her
first, true love waiting with welcoming arms?

Available at your favorite retail outlet. Only from Silhouette Books!

Where love comes alive™

Don't miss the latest miniseries from award-winning author Marie Ferrarella:

Meet...

Sherry Campbell—ambitious newswoman who makes headlines when a handsome billionaire arrives to sweep her off her feet...and shepherd her new son into the world!
A BILLIONAIRE AND A BABY, SE#1528,
available March 2003

Joanna Prescott—Nine months after her visit to the sperm bank, her old love rescues her from a burning house—then delivers her baby....
A BACHELOR AND A BABY, SD#1503,
available April 2003

Chris "C.J." Jones—FBI agent, expectant mother and always on the case. When the baby comes, will her irresistible partner be by her side?
THE BABY MISSION, IM#1220, available May 2003

Lori O'Neill—A forbidden attraction blows down this pregnant Lamaze teacher's tough-woman facade and makes her consider the love of a lifetime!
BEAUTY AND THE BABY, SR#1668,
available June 2003

The Mom Squad—these single mothers-to-be are ready for labor...and true love!

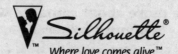

Where love comes alive™

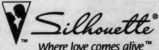